I0709438

The Paranormal Mystery Series

Spirits in Seattle

Paranormal Investigators League Series #6

A Novel
By Deirdre Hutchins

San Joaquin Valley Press
Fresno, California

Spirits in Seattle is published by
San Joaquin Valley Press
P.O. Box 9485
Fresno, CA 93792
www.sanjoaquinvalleypress.com

Cover design by Andria Davis Kaye
The cover is a collage of elements from Shutterstock: Building front by littlenyStock; Hands by Mongolkhon Ake…; Match by hecke 61

ISBN 978-1-7378061-8-9

About Deirdre Hutchins:
Deirdre graduated from Pepperdine University and currently lives in Oregon, where she works as a marketing specialist. When she isn't at her day job, she writes fantasy and ghost stories. She has published 12 books so far and is hard at work on another. Watch for it at the San Joaquin Valley Press website.

Contents

Spirits in Seattle

Chapter 1 – The Olive Nightclub

"I'm pretty sure it's your turn." Anthony looked at his boss Garrett, the owner of the nightclub. Garett sighed. It was after two in the morning and he was ready to head home.

It wouldn't be pretty, but he had to get it over with so he and Anthony could close up for the night. Garrett walked over to the table in the far back corner where Miles often sat listening to the live music and drinking way too many shots. Sure enough, Miles was slumped over on his usual table, lost in alcohol-induced slumber.

"Let's go, Miles," Garrett said as he approached. Miles snored loudly, but otherwise didn't move an inch.

"Miles!" Garrett shouted louder before deciding to give Miles' shoulder a small shove. "Time to go. It's closing time."

The first sign of life, Miles shifted from sleeping on the left side of his face to the right side of his face. Then he snored again. Garrett sighed. At least twice a week Miles came into the Olive Nightclub and ended up passing out drunk somewhere in the club. Garrett was going to have to start cutting him off earlier in the night. This was getting ridiculous. Even though he *was* a great customer.

"Let's go, Miles." Garrett placed one shoulder under Miles' arm and used it to heave Miles to his feet. Barely. Mostly he hung on Garrett's shoulders.

"What? What's happening?" Miles looked around, his dark curls bouncing as he spoke. Garrett wasn't sure, but he assumed Miles was in his late fifties. He'd had a hard life—lost a wife and child, everyone at the Olive pretty much knew that story— and had been a musician himself when he was younger. Before life got in the way. Still, hard life or no, this was taking its toll on Garrett and he was finding it harder and harder to be nice to the old guy.

"Closing time, Miles. Past, even. I'll put you in a cab." Garret began walking, essentially pulling Miles along. Miles was making a lukewarm attempt to walk on his own, but it was ineffective.

Garrett loved this place. He'd been a fairly decent musician back in his younger days also, although he was more Seattle Grunge than the jazz that Miles had played. Still music was music and musicians shared a bond like no other. Being around music every night, not having a typical nine-to-five, seeing people leave his place with joy on their faces...that was all a dream come true for Garrett. Just the occasional annoying drunk patron that stayed past his welcome. It was the only thing that Garrett didn't love about his job as owner of the Olive.

"Back in a flash," Garrett shouted over to Anthony as he carried Miles out the front door.

Anthony continued cleaning up the bar, drying

and putting away the last of the clean glasses, wiping down the bar and barstools. The floors needed to be swept, but the opening crew could do it tomorrow.

He picked up his rag and the cleaning spray and walked over to the nearest table, hoping Garrett would tackle the back tables. He knew it was lazy of him, but he didn't care. He had class in the morning so just wanted to get out of here.

Anthony had just sprayed the tiniest drip of cleaning solution onto the table when he heard a crash behind him. He turned around but didn't see anything. "Garrett?" he called.

"Did you call me?" Garrett asked as he walked back in through the front door of his nightclub. Beads of rain sprinkled his dark blonde hair from the rainy Seattle night.

"Was that you?" Anthony asked.

"Was what me?" Garrett grabbed his own rag and bottle of spray and started cleaning tables near the edge of the stage. It wasn't a large stage, but big enough for a band to play in an intimate setting.

"I heard a crash. Like glass breaking,"

"Huh?" Garrett shrugged. Nothing looked broken. Anthony kept staring at him as if he were denying some big truth. People were always whispering about this place being haunted. He'd never had one experience he couldn't explain and he didn't believe in ghosts. Whispers and rumors didn't make something true. "It was probably me putting Miles in the car."

"It sounded like something breaking at the bar." Anthony walked back over and looked everywhere. Nothing was out of place. No glass shattered anywhere. "So weird. It sounded like it happened right here."

"It's late. You're probably just punch-drunk. Let's finish quickly and get out of here," Garrett instructed and continued cleaning tables.

"Yeah, maybe," Anthony muttered, getting back to cleaning. But he didn't really believe it. "I've got a test tomorrow, so I do want to wrap up."

"Need a ride home?"

"Nah. It's just a few blocks away."

Being located near the University of Washington meant that lots of college students were either patrons or employees of his nightclub. It had been more of an accidental genius rather than some grand strategy, but it had worked out in his favor. Anthony was studying Political Science and was always explaining his philosophy on this policy or that policy. Garrett just listened quietly, but he didn't really care about politics. He was a music guy. He loved freedom, mountain climbing, and living life to the fullest. He didn't really think life was long enough to spend time arguing over policies that helped half the people and angered the other. But he loved the passion Anthony had when he spoke, so he always let him go on and on without interruption.

The door slam made them both jump.

"The wind maybe?" Garrett wondered. It had been sprinkly, but not really storming. He wasn't sure what could have opened and slammed the front door. Anthony didn't even voice what he was thinking, but an uneasiness came over him.

Suddenly, a clunk, clunk, clunk sounded over by the shadowy back corner where Miles had just been sitting down, passed out. They could hear the footsteps but could not see anyone in the darkness.

Anthony sighed a breath of relief. "I guess Miles came back."

It was Garrett's turn to be skeptical. "I put him in the cab myself. And I could've sworn I locked the front door." He dropped the rag on the table he'd been cleaning and slowly started walking toward the shadowy corner where they'd heard Miles' footsteps.

The light didn't really reach this corner very well—it was one of the reasons this area was popular with patrons—but there was enough light to see the outline of tables and chairs, all pushed in and ready for the next night.

Thornbush would be playing tomorrow night. They were a very popular local band.

But the outline of Miles was nowhere to be seen. Garrett walked around a bit more, carefully checking every corner. No Miles.

"There's no one here," Garrett announced, looking around again even as he spoke, in case by some strange chance he'd missed Miles' feet poking out from under a table somewhere.

"But you heard it this time, too, right? Not just me? There was a door slam and footsteps." Anthony was still cleaning, but there was a frantic lilt to his voice. The late night in a dark club was making him believe the worst.

"I'm sure it's just some strange acoustics. You know that's why I bought this place, don't you?" Garrett walked back to the table he'd been cleaning. "The acoustics in this place are fantastic. Perfect for music."

"Yeah. Acoustics. All I know is, I am more motivated than ever to finish cleaning quickly." He sprayed and wiped each table in record time. Garrett just laughed at him. The sounds were strange, for sure, but Anthony's reaction was entertaining to watch.

"No reason to torture you. I can clean the rest

up on my own, if you want to head out," Garrett said, shaking his head and continuing to laugh.

The offer made Anthony embarrassed. He told himself that he just wanted to go because of class in the morning, but the ghost stories associated with this building were definitely playing on a loop in his mind. "No, I can stay. I just want to hurry and finish."

"Suit yourself," Garrett said.

He continued wiping down tables, heading toward the dark corner even as Anthony's path pushed him further away from Miles' favorite spot.

Anthony had just announced his completion when the sound of crying caused them both to freeze.

"Do you hear that?" Anthony asked.

"Yeah. It sounds like a child."

"It sounds like it's coming from the stage," Anthony said, looking behind him. The sound was soft, muffled, but definitely the sound of an upset child. What was a child doing in a nightclub at this late hour?

Garrett gave up cleaning for the night. He felt like the universe was just trying to tell him to head home and clean before opening tomorrow. Peering at the dark stage as he walked, he detoured near the bar so he could drop off the rag and bottle of cleaner. "I don't see anything."

The crying continued, gentle soft sobs as if the child were burying his head in his hands as he cried. Garrett put a little pep in his step as he bounced up onto the stage. He crossed over to the switch on the far left and turned on all the stage lights in one swift movement.

And the crying stopped.

"What was that all about?" Garrett asked, scanning the stage.

"Look behind the drums." Anthony pointed but kept his distance as he instructed his boss.

Garrett made a big show of walking over to the drums and looking behind them. It wouldn't be easy for someone to hide there, but still it was possible. But as Garrett squeezed his head in the space between the drums and the back wall, he saw nothing and no one. He stood up, turned back to Anthony, and shrugged.

"Nothing. I guess it was just the wind."

"The wind again? Dude, your place is haunted." Anthony grabbed his raincoat and shrugged it on as he prepared to leave.

Garrett turned off the stage lights and jumped down off the stage. "You are psyching yourself out. Those rumors aren't true." He walked over to his coat rack and grabbed his own windbreaker, deciding to leave with Anthony.

"I don't know. Sounded pretty real just now to me."

Garrett laughed and started to say, "You're being dramatic..." but the words were cut short, hanging there in the middle of the air. They heard footsteps again, clumping heavily toward the stage.

Their eyes saw nothing.

They watched the stage carefully, their heart rates beginning to increase as the sound of a scuffle occurred and then a loud slap. Anthony startled and Garrett looked over at him in complete wonder. What were they hearing?

And then the child's cries again. This time even louder.

"I think it's coming from under the stage," Anthony whispered. He wasn't sure why he whispered, it just seemed appropriate. Whatever he was hearing, he was convinced it wasn't natural.

Garrett said nothing. He slowly moved forward toward the sound of the cries that were much louder than they had been before, he noticed. Was someone living under his stage and beating on children? He knelt down on all fours in front of the stage and, sure enough, it sounded very much like it was coming from behind the black-painted plywood that covered the front.

"Get me a hammer," he said, pointing at Anthony. Luckily Anthony knew where Garrett kept his tools. Taking in a huge breath of air for courage, he marched into Garrett's office, turning on the light as he did so, and grabbed a hammer from the top of the tool chest that lay on the floor next to Garrett's desk.

Hands shaking, he ran toward Garrett, hammer

first. He wanted to understand what was going on, but at the same time, he was fairly certain he didn't want to know.

Garrett acted quickly, using the bifurcated end to pull the nails out in order to remove the board. He started at the top, working his way down. Just as he'd removed the final nail and went to pull the board back, the crying stopped. Again.

Garrett looked back at Anthony, and Anthony silently shook his head at Garrett. He didn't feel anything good could come of this.

But Garrett was scared that a small child was hurt and stuck under the stage. So, crying or no, he quickly removed the board.

And there he sat. A small, pale little boy with a bowl haircut and strangely out of place clothing. He wore a bowtie—what little kid wears bowties anymore? And Garrett noticed he looked very sickly.

"It's okay. We're here to help." Garrett spoke calmly, slowly.

From behind him, Garrett heard Anthony say,

"This ain't right. This ain't right." Garret ignored him and slowly started to reach a hand toward the frightened young boy.

And the little boy slowly started to reach out to Garrett's outstretched hand. But both Garrett and Anthony watched in horror as the boy slowly changed from pale and sickly, to having no flesh at all. By the time his small hand reached Garrett's, he was a skeleton.

The bony hand touched Garrett's and Garrett recoiled from the feel of bone against his skin.

The boy disappeared and every light went out in the Olive Nightclub at that very moment.

And Garrett and Anthony ran out the front door, not even bothering to lock it behind them.

Chapter 2 – The Wedding

White chairs were set up in neat little rows on the lawn, little lavender bows and white flowers adorning the aisle. Duncan stood at the makeshift altar a few groomsmen behind Greg—a fact Greg hadn't loved—looking out at the sea of faces here to support Paige and Greg on their big day. Duane and Nelson sat together in the second row. Duane had even worn a button-up black shirt to go with his black jeans just for this special occasion.

Duncan had been honored to be in Paige's wedding party, and he couldn't wear a dress. Heck, it wasn't easy to even find a tux his size. So Greg had begrudgingly allowed him to be a groomsman, standing behind Greg's brother-the-best-man and his best friend.

Looking out at the sea of faces, Pachelbel

playing softly in the background, Duncan felt happy for Paige. Sure, he wasn't one hundred percent convinced Greg was good enough for the woman he thought of as a little sister, but he made Paige happy so Duncan went along with it.

There were rows and rows of bushes with tiny flowers on them lining the back of the hotel and shielding most eyes from the main event of the bride's entrance. But most eyes weren't as high as Duncan's, who stood a foot taller than the average wedding guest. He could see everyone as they began their march from the hotel, where they began, before they came into view for others, walking up the aisle of white chairs to the canopy of flowers acting as an altar.

So he smiled softly to himself when he saw Paige before anyone else, standing there all in white, arm in arm with her father.

The first Paranormal Investigators League member to get married.

He looked down at Nelson and Duane sitting in the second row and raised his eyebrows as if to say,

"Can you believe our little Paige is getting married?" And Nelson nodded back to silently respond, "Crazy, right?" Duane tossed his chin in Duncan's direction. He may play the part of being aloof, but Duncan knew well that Duane would also protect Paige like a little sister.

She finally started down the aisle of white chairs, and everyone stood and turned to face Paige. Again, his size allowed him the best view of all and he watched her suck in a deep breath, her eyes locked on Greg's at the end of the aisle, and begin the march toward the altar, her father at her side.

And he couldn't help himself. Duncan stole a thought of how this might change their little dynamic on the team. Paige swore nothing would change, but Greg had already encouraged her to quit once. And he wasn't really sure how the life of a paranormal investigator leant itself to being married. But he forced himself to tuck that thought deep down into his brain for later so he could be present in the moment now.

The ceremony was beautiful, tugged at the

heart strings at just the right times, music playing softly in the background. And Duncan watched it all from a foot above everyone else. Paige's mother cried in the first row. Greg's mother beamed with pride.

And Duncan watched as a very unique blue and yellow butterfly kept circling over Paige and Greg. It made Duncan think of souls of the departed and wondered if that butterfly was a deceased great-aunt or great-grandparent that wanted a front row seat to the whole affair. Too many years hunting ghosts, he supposed. The little ever-present butterfly had the next best view after Duncan himself.

After the ceremony, which was short and to the point, just like Paige herself, the party moved to the ballroom near where Paige had made her bridal entrance at the start of the ceremony. The ballroom was again sprinkled with lavender and white decorations to match the chairs at the ceremony, with the occasional yellow popping up in flowers and accents.

The DJ kept the music lively and upbeat and it

truly felt like a party even as they ate their choice of chicken or steak and listened to toasts from old friends and close family. It was refreshing for Duncan. He rarely got to enjoy the here and now because he spent so much of his life investigating the history of lives lost. He'd almost forgotten that he needed to stop and enjoy his own life every once in a while.

Eventually the lights were dimmed and a disco ball on the ceiling reflected what little light there was, creating sparkles and flashes all over the dance floor. Greg and Paige kicked it off with their first dance to some soft country tune Duncan had never heard before, but it spoke of an incomplete life without the other person. Fitting for a wedding. And right after that, the music turned upbeat again, asking the guests to kick off their shoes and shake a tail feather on the dance floor with the bride and groom.

Duncan wasn't much of a dancer, so he cruised over to where Nelson and Duane sat.

"Fun party, huh?" Duncan raised his glass at Nelson as he grabbed an empty seat at their table and joined the team.

"Yes. It's very Paige," Nelson smiled warmly.

"She does seem happy, even if her new husband is a bit of a dork," Duane grunted.

Duncan shrugged. "I'm a bit of a dork and she's always liked me."

"Do you think she stays with us? Or will she quit again?" Nelson asked.

"I've wondered the same. But who knows?" Duncan shook his head. It seemed they were all wondering how long before Paige put her marriage and family above the team. Again.

As if on cue, Paige bounced over to their table and squeezed in between Duncan and Nelson, hugging both of them at once and pulling them toward her with a strong grip. "My boys!"

Duncan, Nelson and Duane all took turns congratulating her and she beamed in return.

"So, where's the honeymoon?" Duncan asked her.

Paige grabbed the chair on the other side of

Duncan and scooted in. She leaned forward with both elbows on the table and lowered her voice as if she had a big secret. "Seattle."

There was a gleam in her eye as she looked around the table at her ghost-hunting partners. It was as if she were waiting for them to catch on to her practical joke.

"That's a terrible idea. Why wouldn't you go to the Caribbean like normal people?" Duane glared at Paige as he spoke.

"It's certainly...an unusual honeymoon spot, but it's a very beautiful city," Duncan answered.

"Have you ever had a case there, Duncan?" Paige asked, still smiling in a secretive way. Her behavior was definitely making them curious. *What was she going on about?*

"Come to think of it, I can't say that I have," Duncan responded, dragging out each word as if in question to Paige.

"It would be a goldmine," Nelson answered with less curiosity. He was just excited that the topic had gone from honeymoons to haunted locales. "The spiritual activity in that city is supposedly abundant."

Paige clapped her hands and grinned widely. "See? Nelson gets it."

Duncan looked at Nelson, who shook his head. He wasn't quite sure what he was getting.

Duncan turned back to Paige. "Care to enlighten Duane and me?"

Paige leaned back in her chair, her white dress and sparkly tiara making her appear regal. "We have a case in Seattle!"

"Worst honeymoon ever," Duane muttered.

"What are you talking about?" Duncan asked, slowly spacing out every word again.

"I booked my honeymoon in Seattle because I knew we had a case there."

Duncan shook his head. "No, Paige. We'll take the case. You go on your honeymoon."

Paige frowned, her bubble burst. "We are. In Seattle. We're going to do both at once." She scooted her seat closer to Duncan. "It's a nightclub. The owner,

Garrett, saw the ghost of a little boy who keeps crying. Apparently, there've been rumors about the place for years."

"Hmmm... Child ghost.   Intriguing," Nelson answered, but Duncan held up his hands.

"It sounds like a great case, but not for your honeymoon, Paige."

"Duncan, I can do both, I promise. Whenever we're not working, Greg and I can go around the city and see the sights." Paige smiled again with her usual twinkle in her eye.

"And Greg has okayed this?" Duncan asked skeptically, one eyebrow higher than the other.

Paige fanned the air in front of her. "Greg thinks it's great."

As if on cue, Greg came up behind Paige's chair and rested his hands on its back. "What do I think is great?"

"Our honeymoon in Seattle.   Right, honey?" Paige asked, a little too eagerly.

"Oh, yeah." His whole body language changed

from stiff to energetic and even a bit giddy. He was usually a fairly "stiff" person, but suddenly he was bouncing with energy just like his new wife. "I'm really excited to try out this ghost-hunting thing. Never much believed in them myself, but Paige says the experience will make me a believer. Thanks for letting me join in." Someone across the room caught his eye. "Aunt Margaret!" He leaned in and kissed Paige on the cheek. "Be back in a bit for another dance, *Mrs. Parker*."

And he walked off to greet his guests while Paige looked at her team with imploring eyes.

"Absolutely not," Duane stated without moving from his slouched position in his seat.

"So that was your plan? To make the case in Seattle the actual honeymoon?" Duncan asked.

"Very efficient of you, Paige." Nelson nodded his head in her direction.

"Thank you, Nelson." Paige nodded back.

"No, we are not encouraging this." Duncan looked back at Nelson.

"Why not?" Paige asked.

"Because it's a terrible idea," Duane answered.

Duncan sighed. "You should have a real honeymoon, Paige. It's an important part of a new marriage. Or so I hear."

"This is who I am and what I love to do. And I want to share it with my new husband." Paige shrugged. "I think it's the perfect way to get him to support this part of my life. He'll see why it's so important to all of us."

"Guaranteed he cries at least once during the investigation," Duane stated.

"He's not going to cry, Duane." Paige rolled her eyes at her teammate.

"Against my better judgment, I'm going to agree to this bizarre request. But *only* because it's your wedding day and because it is nice to have you on cases. But—" Duncan held a finger up in front of Paige. "—if he gets in the way or causes any problems, he's out."

"Oh, thank you, Duncan!" And she flung her

arms around Duncan's large neck.

"And if at any point on the case you decide you want a real honeymoon, you already have our blessing," Duncan added.

"You won't regret this, Duncan. It's going to be great. You'll see." Paige stood up and bounced on her toes as she often did when she was excited.

"You know," Nelson said, adjusting his glasses, "your plan could backfire egregiously, Paige. You very well know this life isn't for everyone."

Paige just shook her head at Nelson. "Come on, Nelson. Dance with me."

Nelson looked frightened, so Duncan leaned in. "You can't say no to a bride on her wedding day."

"That's right. You can't." She held a hand out toward Nelson and he begrudgingly slipped his own hand in. She led him to the dance floor, she bouncing to the beat as she walked and he marching off with heavy feet as if to an execution.

Duncan just laughed as he watched them.

Duane moved from his seat to the one Nelson

had been in moments ago. "If I see them kiss while we're working, I will puke."

Duncan placed a large hand on Duane's shoulder. "I trust Paige to be completely professional."

Duane frowned. "It's not Paige I'm worried about."

"I do think this is going to be a case to remember."

Duane just curled his lip in disgust as a response and they continued watching Paige trying to teach Nelson how to dance on the dance floor. And it was a ridiculous sight.

But also endearing.

The dynamic might have changed, but Duncan was willing to give it a go. Because their team might be quirky, but they meant everything in the world to him.

Chapter 3 – The Emerald City

"So what do we investigate first?" Greg asked, his suitcase still in his hand as the Paranormal Investigators League gathered in the lobby of their hotel. Since it was also Greg and Paige's honeymoon, they stepped up their game and stayed at a luxury hotel on Pine Street near the famous Pike Place Market. Normally, Duncan would have booked the cheapest dive motel he could find.

"There's no 'we.' Only Duncan and Paige meet with the client," Duane sneered.

Duncan held a hand up to keep the peace. "While I do appreciate the enthusiasm, Greg, there's not much for you to do just yet. Why don't you and Paige take the day and see the city? Nelson and I can meet with the client."

"Really, Duncan?" Paige grabbed Greg's arm

and squeezed, her smile wide and buoyant.

"If we're going to give you the world's weirdest honeymoon, it's the least I can do," Duncan smiled back.

"Thanks, Dunk." Greg slapped Duncan's arm in a way that said they were better friends than they were, but for Paige's sake Duncan ignored the nickname he already hated. "What do you think about heading to the Space Needle, Paige?" Greg continued.

"I love it." Paige, still grinning, leaned in and kissed her new husband.

Duane groaned.

"We'll meet back here at midnight for the investigation," Duncan instructed.

"See ya at midnight." Paige smiled and walked arm in arm with Greg toward the elevators so they could drop off their luggage.

Duane grunted a response which Duncan assumed was in the affirmative before he also walked away.

Duncan turned to Nelson. "You ready?"

Nelson adjusted his glasses. He looked stiff, uncomfortable. "Absolutely. But do you think I'm ready to be in front of clients?"

Duncan folded his arms. "Why wouldn't you be?"

"I'm not really a 'people-person.' I don't exactly have Paige's personality."

Duncan half-smiled. "No one has Paige's personality. Come on, this part is easy. We just have to get firsthand accounts of their experiences at the Olive. Think of it as research. You're really good with that."

"Research. Got it."

Nelson followed Duncan back out to Duncan's beat-up old Chevy. How it was still running after all the years it had seen was a mystery to everyone. The sky was hazy and a light drizzle filled the air. It wasn't enough to make windshield wipers necessary, but enough to give everything a layer of moisture. The day was cool, but definitely not cold. It actually felt refreshing to Duncan.

They drove east toward the university until

they came to the nondescript building where the Olive Nightclub was located. Duncan was surprised to find a parking place right in front. As Duncan turned off the engine, they both glanced at the brown stone façade. There was a flat neon sign announcing the location and a heavy, thick front door. It didn't look like what Duncan pictured a happening nightclub to look like.

"I'll never understand the appeal of a place like this," Nelson announced.

"You know. It's a place where college students can come blow off steam. You went to college. You remember."

Nelson just stared at Duncan.

"Well, you've heard of people doing it, right?"

"Yeah, I know people frequent places like this. I just don't get it personally." Nelson looked back up at the brown building. "I wonder what this building was prior. It looks like it's seen some days on this earth."

"And now you're doing your job. You and Paige can look that very question up tomorrow." Duncan frowned, remembering that Paige was really here on her honeymoon. "Or maybe you can."

"I will." Nelson nodded while Duncan opened his door and climbed out. Nelson followed right behind.

Duncan reached his hand toward the handle and the heavy front door of the Olive opened suddenly.

"Oh, you're here. Come on in." Garrett smiled as he opened the door for the investigators. Duncan loved Garrett's look from the moment he saw him, as if they were kindred souls in the world of fashion. His hair was long and shaggy, and his clothes looked like a garage sale find. Other than his goatee, he looked like a page out of Duncan's book.

"I'm Duncan and this is Nelson. We're the Paranormal Investigators League," Duncan introduced.

"Garrett." the blonde man gestured to himself and then inside toward his bar. "Come in."

The room was sunken, and Duncan and Nelson followed Garrett down the few steps into the dimly lit bar and nightclub. An intimate stage filled the wall at the other end of the room and the open space was filled with small tables and round-backed chairs. Half a dozen people or so were hanging out at the bar.

"This is my staff. They all have stories to tell so they wanted to be here," Garrett explained.

"That's great." Duncan smiled, truly meaning it. The more stories that they could gather, the easier their job would be.

"So what now?" Garrett asked.

"My case manager told me that you saw a bony hand. Can you tell me the story in your own words and show me where it happened?" Duncan asked.

"Oh, yeah. It was so weird. And I don't even really believe in any of all this stuff." Garrett started walking toward the stage. "There have been rumors about this place as long as I can remember, but I never had one single personal experience until two weeks ago. Anthony was here too."

Garrett gestured back toward his staff standing around the bar. Duncan assumed Anthony was the guy who swallowed hard with wide eyes like he'd...well, like he'd seen a ghost.

Garrett continued his story. "We kept hearing weird sounds like footsteps and such. And crying. We kept hearing a child crying. I naturally assumed an alive child was really here. So when we pinpointed the sound to beneath the stage, Anthony and I removed the front panel and saw a boy in old-style clothing hiding under there. He was scared."

"Can you give a general timeframe to the clothing?" Duncan asked.

Garrett tightened his lips in thought. "Maybe early 1900's? I'm not great with the history of fashion. But he had a bowtie and it looked old-fashioned."

"How did you know it was a ghost and not just a scared boy?" Nelson asked.

Garrett's eyes widened as he remembered the night. "I didn't at first. But when he reached out to me, his hand turned to a skeleton. It was like...like under the stage he's a boy and if he leaves the cover of the stage he turns to a skeleton." Garrett shook his head. "I know. It sounds so weird."

"Not really," Nelson answered but said nothing

more.

So Duncan added, "We've heard worse."

Garrett laughed an uncomfortable laugh. "Good."

"Is that your only experience?" Duncan asked.

Garrett shook his head. "It's my only experience seeing anything, but we hear the crying almost every night now."

"And glasses keep breaking," a young woman with her green hair coming out of a beanie and a hoop through her left nostril shouted out to them.

"That's right, Willow," Garrett snapped as he remembered. "Almost every night we lose at least one glass. That's getting annoying."

"They just fly off the bar, or what?" Duncan asked.

"We don't always see it, but I think Willow did once. Right?"

The girl with the green hair nodded and then responded, "I was tending bar that night and we were packed. I think it was the night Thornbush played."

"Thornbush is popular with the college crowd," Garrett explained.

"I pulled two glasses down and went to pour, but before I could, one glass slid to the edge and shattered on the floor. It looked like I was just being klutzy, but I know it wasn't me." Willow shook her head.

Duncan nodded. He'd heard similar stories at other cases.

"And we hear the sound of glass shattering, even when we don't see any evidence of it at all," the girl named Willow added. "We hear it all the time."

Garrett added, "I don't believe in ghosts, but I can't really explain what I saw."

"Well," Duncan smiled, "I admire your dedication to your beliefs."

"The kinetic energy from the manifestation of a spirit can easily cause objects to move or sounds to be made," Nelson explained.

"Everyone knows this place is haunted," the young man Duncan believed to be Anthony said. He shook his head. "But hearing those cries and seeing that bony hand? No way. That was one hundred percent a ghost."

"This place is really creepy," Willow added.

"I just ask, no matter what, for some discretion," Garrett said, stepping closer to Duncan. "I've poured my life savings into this place and I can't afford for rumors to ruin that."

"Rumors? I thought you saw something?" Duncan asked.

"Well, I don't know what I saw." Garrett frowned.

"You saw a ghost, Garrett. I saw it too," Anthony answered.

"Believe me, you wouldn't be the first business owner worried about how a haunting or a rumor of a haunting could hurt their profits. We've dealt with it before," Duncan explained. This seemed to calm Garrett somewhat. "We'll do everything in our power to get to the bottom of this, whatever the situation may be. And only you will share our findings with the world. Or not. But I will say, having a haunted business isn't always a deterrent."

"Has anyone else had an experience?" Nelson asked the staff near the bar.

Every hand shot straight in the air.

"I've heard the crying," one staff member said.

"Footsteps."

"The lights on the stage go on and off by themselves."

Duncan asked, "Any other sightings of the entity besides Garrett and Anthony?"

One small hand went timidly in the air. It belonged to a small blonde woman who barely looked of legal age to be working in a bar.

"Can you describe what you saw?" Duncan encouraged with a soothing voice. The girl looked like a frightened animal who might run at the slightest sound.

"I saw the boy being choked by a large man," she said in a soft, shaky voice.

"What did the man look like?" Duncan asked.

This was the first they'd heard of another entity.

The girl shook her head. "They were both in shadow. I saw the vision behind the stage." And with a shaky finger she pointed at the stage. Duncan turned over his shoulder cautiously, partially expecting to see the large shadow choking the small boy. He saw nothing.

"Did you know about this?" Duncan asked Garrett.

Garrett shrugged. "Like I said, there are tons of rumors about this place. I never really believed any of them."

"So I assume if we do find evidence of a spirit, or spirits, you want them exorcised?"

Garrett nodded. "Yeah. I want this all over with so we can go back to the way it was. Music, drinks, and fun. Where the rumors are only rumors."

"Understood." Duncan clapped his hands together. "Then we'll investigate tonight and get you some answers."

"What do you do?" Anthony asked.

"We set up cameras, try to talk to the ghosts, see if we can find non-paranormal explanations for what you experienced. That kind of thing. We've done it plenty of times before," Duncan explained.

"No. I mean," Anthony continued, "what do you do if you're dealing with something evil?"

Duncan frowned. "Well, sadly, we've dealt with that too."

Chapter 4 - Late Night at the Olive

"We definitely need a camera facing the stage," Duncan instructed as Duane continued setting up equipment.

"Where do you want me with the handheld?" Nelson asked.

"I think on the stage, if you don't mind."

Nelson smiled meekly. "That'll be my first time on a stage."

"Really?" At Nelson's nod, Duncan continued, "Well, you'd better get used to it for all your future TED talks."

"Is there anything I can do to help?" Garrett asked. His staff had gone home, but he had decided to stay for the investigation. While rare, it wasn't unheard of and Duncan was comfortable with a client's decision either way. And he understood. The Olive was Garrett's livelihood.

"Yeah." Duncan looked behind himself. "Can you grab that bottle of baby powder and sprinkle it all over the bar?"

"I'm sorry. Do what now?"

"It's a typical test we do. Sprinkle the baby powder on the bar and put a couple glasses in the middle. If they slide around, you'll see the evidence even if none of us happen to be looking when it happens." Duncan looked over his other shoulder. "In fact, didn't you say you heard footsteps in that back corner?"

Garrett nodded as he confirmed.

"Then I suggest we sprinkle some over there too. That way we can catch footprints if the spirit walks over there."

"I'm going to use this back table as the command post," Duane announced to Duncan as he placed his laptop on the corner table that Miles always passed out on. "That way we leave the bar area free for investigating."

"Yeah, that works," Duncan responded. Duane would often use a client's kitchen when they were in a home, but in a place like this where it was all one big room, he really just needed to be out of the way.

The front door was flung open abruptly and Duncan was surprised to see that tiny little Paige had been the one to push it open. It was a very heavy door. Then again, he well knew that what she lacked in size she made up for in boundless energy.

"Where do you want us?" Paige asked as she bounced in, Greg right behind her. To his credit, he looked curious and mildly interested, which Duncan found surprising. He'd half expected Greg to talk Paige out of coming tonight.

"If you're okay with it, I was thinking perhaps under the stage. I'd do it but...," Duncan responded, holding his hands out to indicate that his size wasn't conducive to under the stage investigating. "I think there could be an opportunity for some great EVPs."

"Yeah, that sounds awesome." Paige practically skipped over to Duncan to grab the audio recorder from him. Greg followed her over to Duncan.

"How are you with a camera?" Duncan asked Greg as he held out a small handheld video recorder.

"Wow. Old school," Greg laughed as he grabbed it from Duncan.

"High end. And very good with little to no light. Just keep panning all around beneath the stage in case you see the ghost boy."

Greg raised an eyebrow. "Ghost boy?"

"Yes. Apparently, he sometimes cries under the stage and Garrett even saw him once." Duncan gestured at Garrett, who was at the bar sprinkling the baby powder in a very light coating.

"Oh, no. You've got to really cover it. Let me show you." Paige went behind the bar and turned the baby powder bottle upside down so a generous helping covered the bar top. "It has to be thick if you want definitive proof."

Greg looked awkwardly up at Duncan, holding the camera loosely in his hands. "Thanks for letting us join you. I know it means a lot to Paige."

"I should be thanking you. I know Paige loves ghost-hunting, but this is really out of the ordinary."

"Well, if I want to know everything about her, I guess I have to start here."

"That much is true." Duncan went back to set-up mode. "Now the space under the stage is small, so if you need to get out every few minutes to stretch your back, feel free."

"Okay. And Duncan?"

Duncan responded by raising both his eyebrows.

"What if I see a ghost?"

"Oh. Then keep filming."

"Is that what you guys do?"

"That's exactly what we do. We capture evidence of the paranormal. The more the merrier. Listen, this is a child ghost. Probably some eerie crying but that's about it. It'll be a good case for your first time out."

"First case? So I might get to join you again sometime?" Greg asked, a small smile creeping across his face.

"If you're even half as good at this as Paige, you'll be begging me for more cases. Now go get in place. Almost time for lights out." Duncan waved an arm toward the stage.

"Do *all* the lights go out?" Greg asked.

"Yes. It doesn't need to be dark for a ghost to appear. We just find it easier to capture them that way." He turned back to Paige, who was now helping Garrett sprinkle baby powder in the dark corner behind Duane's command post. "You ready for lights out, Paige?"

"Always." She looked up from the corner where she was pointing for Garrett to sprinkle. "Do you want this whole walkway? Or is this good enough?"

Duncan walked across the nightclub in a few large steps and inspected what they had so far. A thick layer of powder covered the walkway behind Duane almost halfway to the stage. "This will do." He turned to Duane, who was now sitting at the table in front of his laptop, checking all the camera views that were transmitting. "Duane, just watch this behind you and be careful not to step in it."

"Why would I?" Duane peeled his eyes from the laptop long enough to glare at Duncan.

"Ready for lights out?" Duncan asked, ignoring Duane's antics.

"Ready." Duane answered simply.

"Nelson? Ready?" Duncan called to the stage where Nelson was already pacing. In response, Nelson simply held up a single thumb.

Duncan turned back to Paige. "Let's get into position."

Paige nodded as she bounced over to the stage, grabbing Greg and pulling him underneath with her. Because of her small stature, she was able to sit up with her back fairly straight. Greg, however, was hunched in a ball and didn't look like he was excited to be there anymore. Paige squeezed his hand and smiled. In contrast, she was barely holding her excitement in.

"Where do you want me?" Garrett asked, holding out the baby powder bottle.

"You're with me." Duncan gestured over his shoulder. "We'll be over near the bar." They weaved between tables and got into position, Garrett seated at a barstool and Duncan standing nearby. Duncan preferred to stand so he could pace and inspect as they investigated. When it looked like they were all ready to go, Duncan shouted, "Lights out."

Duane complied by turning out the main nightclub overhead lights and Nelson turned out the lights that were used to light up the stage. A tiny sliver of light crept in from the front windows where a streetlamp stood, but otherwise the Olive was dark. Almost pitch black in places like underneath the stage.

At other investigations they used walkie-talkies to communicate, but here it was easy enough for them to all hear each other simply by raising their voices. The Olive Nightclub was an intimate venue.

Greg startled when Paige began speaking into the darkness. "Is there a spirit of a little boy nearby?"

She waited for a response she couldn't hear, hoping that if they got an answer the recorder would pick up what their ears couldn't. Then she asked another question, speaking into the void of the darkness, "If there is anyone here with us, can you show us? Give us a sign."

Greg held his breath as he waited for the sign Paige requested. It never came. They sat there in silence and darkness, listening and waiting. For some reason, Greg found his heart pounding in anticipation. Did he actually believe there was a ghost living under the stage? The idea seemed preposterous, and yet he was nervous.

Duncan paced. Nelson inspected. Garrett twirled the baby bottle powder. Duane watched it all from his table in the dark corner. Minutes in the darkness felt interminable.

"Nothing may happen," Garrett announced. "I've been here many late nights by myself and nothing ever happened."

Duncan sighed before answering. "Yeah.

Believe me, we know ghosts aren't like trained dogs to perform on command. Sometimes we wait around all night for a whole lot of nuthin."

"But?" Garrett asked, assuming there was sometimes more or Duncan wouldn't have a job.

"But sometimes, we get a whole lotta sumpin."

Paige's voice rang out from under the cramped stage. "Is there anyone here with us who wants to make their presence known? Are you the one who keeps hurting little boys?"

Duncan heard a thump behind Duane just as Duane pulled his headphones off. He spoke calmly as he stated, "Duncan. I got something over here."

Aiming his handheld toward Duane, Duncan walked and filmed. "I heard it."

Another thump sounded. And then another. It sounded like really spaced-out footsteps. And as Duncan passed Duane, he panned the camera across the baby powder. It was easier to see on the infrared of the camera than with the naked eye in the dark nightclub. "Well, I'll be."

"What?" Garrett came up behind Duncan. Instead of answering, Duncan pointed at the baby powder trail Garrett himself had made. There, right in the middle, was a large footprint, the size and shape of someone wearing a thick, heavy boot. And it was so central, it didn't look like anyone could make it easily without doing some serious jumping and landing on one foot.

And everything stopped. No more thumps, no more footprints.

"Paige," Duncan called. "Keep going on the accusatory path. I think you were on to something."

Even though Duncan couldn't see her from where he stood, Paige popped her head out from under the stage and said, "Got it." As she got back into position under the stage she said to Greg, "Ready to make it mad, honey?"

Greg shrugged and said "Sure." He wasn't thrilled with the cramped space and the utter darkness, but forcing something exciting to happen? That sounded interesting.

Paige put the recorder near her mouth and asked, "Do you like to hurt children? Does it make you feel tough to hurt those weaker than you?"

A low growl sounded in Paige's ear. She figured it wasn't Greg, but she asked him to be sure. "That wasn't you, was it?"

"Not me. What was it?" Greg's senses were on high alert. The growl had been very clear.

"I don't know." Paige popped out from under the stage again. "We heard a growl over here, Duncan."

"Oh, nice!" Duncan responded. "No further experiences over here yet. Keep going."

Without hesitation, Paige continued provoking whatever had growled in her ear. "Was that you growling at me? So you like to pick on women and children? A big tough guy, huh?"

This time the response wasn't as subtle.

Footsteps overhead stomped across the stage causing the instruments that were housed there to rattle. Drums shook. Guitars vibrated. Nelson panned his camera, sweeping right and left, but saw nothing other than shaking instruments. Paige listened as the stage above her shook in time with the thumping steps. They were loud, heavy thumps, the sound someone makes when they are a large person or someone very angry. Or both.

"Did you note the time, Duane?" Nelson called out into the darkness, even as he kept his eyes on the stage he was filming.

"Noted," Duane called out. To Duncan he said, more even keeled, "Sounds like Paige really set this one off."

"Yeah, she's good at that," Duncan responded, slowly starting to move toward the stage, taking the side walkway so he wouldn't have to weave between tables, but being careful not to step on the layer of baby powder. "Now we are getting somewhere."

"Why don't you pick on someone your own size? Are you a coward?" Paige asked, calling into the darkness.

As if to punctuate her words, the footsteps thumped to the front of the stage and then stopped as suddenly as they'd begun. The investigators knew it might be over, or it might be just getting started. But Greg had no frame of reference, so he relaxed enough to let out a small chuckle. Paige was still holding her breath waiting to see what happened next, so without making a sound she squeezed Greg's leg. She hoped he'd interpret it as a sign to be quiet and wait. He didn't catch the hint.

"I think you scared him." Greg had laughter in his voice.

And then Greg screamed.

Paige could only make out shapes and outlines in the darkness as she watched an unseen hand grab Greg and slide him unwillingly out from under the stage. He slid on his butt across the floor in front of the stage and stopped only when he crashed into the table and chairs closest to the stage.

Duncan ran to him to make sure he was okay and Paige scrambled out from under the dark stage. She hadn't gotten very far when something grabbed her foot.

"Duncan?" she said, her voice thick with tension.

"Yeah?" Duncan asked as he laid a hand on Greg to make sure he was unharmed. But he never got an answer from Paige before she slid, pulled by her feet back under the stage. "Paige?"

It was dark and Duncan wasn't completely confident he saw what he thought he saw, but Paige didn't appear to be anywhere. He turned his cell phone light on and knelt in front of the stage. "Paige?"

"Where is she?" Greg's voice was laced with panic. His jovial, nonchalant demeanor was erased in an instant. "Duncan? What's going on?"

Duncan was slightly worried that he didn't see Paige, but he didn't want to contribute to the panic. "I think she got pulled back under the stage."

"By what?" Greg asked with a shaky voice, but Duncan didn't reply. He didn't know what they were dealing with yet, but they had dealt with powerful beings before. He trusted Paige knew how to handle herself.

Kneeling down as low as he could go, Duncan stuck his head in the small opening under the stage that Paige had been coming and going from. There was no way Duncan could get more than a head in there. "Paige?"

Silence was his response. He strained his eyes as far as he could see with the little light from his phone, but there was nothing to see or hear. "Nelson? I need you to go in there after her. I'm too big."

"Of course," Nelson said, walked to the edge of the stage and hopped down in a swifter movement than Duncan had ever seen.

"What's going on, Duncan?" Greg asked again, concern bordering on panic still overtaking his tone.

Duncan ran a hand through his long bangs as he mulled over Greg's question. He had always been a straight shooter so he figured no reason to start sugarcoating now. "I don't know," he answered honestly.

"Hold this." Nelson handed the handheld to Duncan and got on all fours. The opening beneath the stage swallowed Nelson into darkness as he crawled in.

And then they heard a small voice. "Duncan?" No denying it was Paige.

"Paige," Duncan stuck his head in again as he called out to her. "Talk to me, Paige."

"I need a handheld. Now." There was no fear, but definitely a sense of urgency.

Following her request, Duncan handed the handheld back to Nelson, who was still just inside the opening, and he took it.

"Nelson's bringing it to you now. Where are you?" Duncan called into the darkness beneath the stage.

"Way in the back. There's a hallway of some sort. And Duncan?" Paige called back.

"Yeah?"

"There isn't just one ghost boy. There are dozens."

Nelson looked back at Duncan as Duncan urged him forward. "Go." This they needed to have on camera.

As Nelson crawled beneath the stage toward Paige, Duncan stood back up and ran back to where Duane sat at his command post. He'd be able to see everything on Paige's feed. Greg and Garrett followed and all three crowded in behind Duane.

True to his nature, Duane said nothing, just pointed at the small window that showed that particular feed. And they watched as Nelson crawled under the stage, mostly just seeing nothing and an occasional wooden post holding up the stage.

When Nelson made it to the clearing, Duncan saw grainy footage with a slightly green tint to it which meant there was very little light. Nelson stood and panned up Paige's stock-still body. She didn't dare move because several boys in 1900-era, turn-of-the-century clothing were gathering around her and reaching out to her clothes and hair. They seemed to be as in awe of her as she was of them.

"Whoa," was all Nelson could say.

"Is that...real?" Greg asked, watching his newlywed wife through the screen and infrared footage.

"It's something," Duncan responded.

"Nelson, come help me," Paige instructed and Nelson obeyed. He walked over to her and extended his hand, allowing her to pull free of the gathering boys. They watched her closely but stopped reaching out for her.

Nelson wasn't sure if she wanted to leave or not, but Paige answered his thoughts by getting to work. She asked the boys, "Who are you? What do you want?"

They stared at her with empty eyes. Their cheeks were sunken and their skin pale, barely visible as they were in the low light. They each looked like an independent person, but they matched each other in a way that seemed robot-like. They swayed, reached, moved in unison. Almost like they were cogs in some kind of giant machine.

Paige asked the question most burning her mind. "What happened to you?"

Wordlessly, they pointed all in unison, raising

their arms at the same time and pace, aiming their extended pointer fingers to behind where they all stood. Paige followed the sight line with her eyes, straining in the dark. What was hard to see in the low light was much easier for Duncan, Garrett, Greg and Duane to see on the laptop. Against the back wall was a large dark figure.

It swiped a large, looming arm toward the boys and they all instantly disappeared.

Nelson continued to film the empty hallway, but it was quiet and peaceful yet again. He looked at Paige, who shrugged in return.

"What was that all about?"

Greg took that opportunity to run to the stage and call for Paige. When Nelson and Paige emerged from under the stage, Greg asked her, "What the hell was that? Those boys. That shadow thing. This means this place is haunted, right?"

Paige looked into the darkness to confirm the answer with Duncan, but she couldn't see him from where she stood. He was too deep into the shadows across the nightclub. So she went with her years of experience. "Unless this place is filled with a strange sort of magic, yes. Those were ghosts."

Chapter 5 – Brethren Reform School

"It was too intense." Greg was pacing their hotel room that overlooked the Sound. The Ferris wheel that adorned the pier was visible in the distance. A haze of clouds littered the sky. But it wasn't raining. Yet.

"I'll admit it was a bit more dramatic than we often see during an investigation. We usually don't even know there was a spirit with us until we review the footage. Which Duane will be doing today." Paige was loading her bag. She and Nelson had plans to go meet with a local historian later that day.

"Duncan said we could have some time to ourselves." Greg grabbed Paige's arms, none too gently, and then realized his error and began rubbing her arms. "Can't we just not ghost-hunt for one day?"

Paige frowned. She'd hoped he'd fall in love

with it just as she had, but clearly that hadn't been the case. Of course, he *had* been thrown on his very first case. That would rattle anyone. "Greg, this is what I do." She shook her head. "I wouldn't be able to enjoy the day with all the questions running through my head. Don't you want to know who those boys were and why their spirits are still stuck in the nightclub for all eternity?"

Greg dropped his hold on Paige's arms and sighed. He might not share her passion, but he could respect that she *was* passionate. "Well then, can I come with you? I don't really want to go to Pike Place without you."

Paige squealed and jumped up to wrap her arms around his neck. She knew he was just doing it to make her happy, but it worked. She was happy. She had delusions of him joining their cases every now and again so they could share the stories and the experiences. It wasn't exactly turning out as she'd hoped, but a little give and take was good. For now. That was marriage, after all, right?

"Let me just call Nelson and tell him. I'm sure he won't mind," Paige said as she pulled her phone out of her back pocket and called her fellow investigator. As she explained the new plan to Nelson, Greg thought about the case and the boys stuck below a nightclub stage. But then he realized he was far more curious about the dark entity with the heavy footsteps. The one that threw him and yanked Paige. That all the ghost boys were afraid of.

That's where this case is going to end up, he thought.

"All set. As I suspected Nelson was totally fine with it. Let me just finish grabbing my supplies." Paige turned back to packing her over-sized shoulder bag as Greg sat on the bed, watching her.

"Yeah, he seems like a nice guy."

"They all are." Paige continued stuffing items into her bag, carefully setting the digital voice recorder she always carried in a zippered pouch for instant discoverability when she needed it. "Even Duane. He comes off gruff, but it's all an act. Deep down he's a big softy too."

"So what is his story? He seems miserable."

Paige stopped packing and looked out the window. Duane had been through a lot, but he didn't like to show his emotions. He'd lost a sister years ago and the guilt still haunted him more than ghosts ever could. But that felt too personal to tell Greg on Duane's behalf. "He's dealt with some things. Things that would make anyone a bit sulky."

Greg huffed a laugh. "Sulky. That's a good word for it."

Paige lifted her bag over her shoulder. "Honestly, if he wore a bright red shirt and smiled at me, I might keel over in shock. His moodiness is part of his charm."

Greg swallowed down the jealousy. She was the only female on this investigating team and it was clear she loved her teammates. But Greg reminded himself that she had married *him*. He told himself her relationship with the ghost investigators was just work-related.

"Shall we?" Paige gestured toward the front door when Greg continued sitting on the bed and not catching the clue she gave when putting her bag on her shoulder. "I'd like to grab a coffee in the lobby before we head out."

Greg raised an eyebrow. "When in Rome?"

"Something like that." Paige left the hotel room and Greg followed her down to the lobby.

A short while later, Nelson caught up with them and Paige handed him a coffee. Greg again couldn't help but feel a twinge of jealousy. Paige never really drank coffee at home—especially not the frou-frou five-dollar kind—and here she was indulging *and* knowing Nelson's drink order in advance.

"Oh, thank you, Paige. I needed this." Nelson nodded a greeting at Greg. "I never sleep all that well after an active investigation. Too many 'what-ifs' running through my mind."

"That's what I said," Paige answered. "What is the story with all those kids?"

Greg took a chance and voiced his own

thoughts. "And who is the scary puppeteer that threw me?"

Nelson pointed at Greg. "Exactly. He's like some evil ringleader or something. And I want to know the full story."

"Once you know the story, what do you do with it?" Greg asked. While he was as curious as the rest of them, he didn't yet quite connect the dots on what difference that made.

"Ghosts are usually spirits with unfinished business. Sometimes it's as simple as helping them get closure so they can cross over," Paige explained, bouncing on the balls of her feet as she explained the thing she loved most in the world.

"And other times?" Greg raised an eyebrow.

Nelson and Paige exchanged a look.

"Sometimes it takes a little more," Paige answered cryptically.

But Nelson couldn't take the hint and continued with more color. "We've done séances, Voodoo, exorcisms, witchcraft...whatever it takes."

"I'm sorry. What?" Greg laughed nervously.

"The spiritual world doesn't pigeonhole itself like humans do, Greg. You gotta do what works," Nelson explained matter-of-factly.

At the sight of Greg's shocked face, Paige decided it was best to change the subject before he did something dramatic she didn't like. Like demand that they leave immediately before any witchcraft was performed. "Shall we go visit the historian and get some answers?"

Paige over-smiled, hoping her enthusiasm would shift the mood.

"I'm ready. Absolutely on the edge of my seat, actually," Nelson answered.

Greg followed, watching Paige, but saying nothing. He was struggling to wrap his mind around the cute, bubbly brunette he'd married and the dabbling in the occult that Nelson had just rattled off.

He had so much to learn about investigating hauntings.

They chatted on the drive to meet with the

historian, talking about frivolous stuff and avoiding the previous night's events entirely. Greg wasn't sure if he liked that or hated it, but he followed the conversation. He'd always been a sociable person.

The building Nelson parked the P.I.L. van in front of was not at all what any of them had been expecting of a historical center. They'd met with their share of local historians in their time and usually it was in a museum or a historical home maintained by a local preservation society. This was a modern building with large windows and sharp angles. And behind it was Lake Union in all her natural glory.

"Wow," Paige said as they climbed out of the van.

"Yeah. I guess this is the New Age historical society," Nelson responded, shielding his eyes from the glare of what little sun was shining through the clouds and bouncing off the top of the lake.

"Let's go," Paige instructed and led the group to the main entrance. The front door was glass, like the whole front exterior, and they could see all the way in before they'd even arrived. Inside were desks with a few papers, but nothing like what they were used to with mountains of books and documents. Paige opened the door and a gentleman in a gray business suit met them immediately.

"You must be the Paranormal Investigators League," he said with a warm smile.

There were people here and there hunched over keyboards and focusing intently on computer screens. Very modern. Not at all what Paige and Nelson typically stumbled upon with historians.

"I'm Paige," Paige nodded in response and then pointed behind her. "And this is Nelson and Greg." She looked around at the high ceilings and the view of Lake Union through the back windows. "Nice setup you got here."

"Do you like it? We got a large grant about five years ago and used it to really modernize our operations. We keep all of our historical records on digital backup now. Much faster to find anything we need than the old-school card catalogs."

"I believe it," Paige responded.

"I'm Luther, by the way." He extended his hand and they each shook it with the appropriate nice-to-meet-you greeting. Luther led them down a short hallway and into a conference room that was again completely floor-to-ceiling windows on the lake side. With the sun beginning to peek through the clouds, it was shaping up to be a beautiful Pacific Northwest day.

"So what can I help you with? A ghost story?" He smiled in conspiratorial glee. Paige sighed in response. Just another campfire ghost story to entertain the kids. Some people had no clue the real lives that hauntings often ruined or complicated.

But Nelson was oblivious to the sentiment and so he answered, "Yes. The Olive Nightclub has reported some disturbances, and we were wondering if you could tell us a bit about its history?"

Paige dug through her bag. "I found out it used to be an apartment building, but the details in public records didn't go back much before 1920. We need the history for the late 1800's to early 1900's." She handed the pile of printed papers she'd pulled out of her bag over to Luther.

He studied them cursorily before his eyes went wide. "Oh. You mean the site of the Brethren Fire."

"What was the Brethren Fire?" Nelson asked immediately, adjusting his black-rimmed glasses as he leaned forward across the conference room.

"1896, I believe. There was a boys' school, a reform school. It completely burned to the ground one night and all the children died." Luther leaned back in his chair as he relayed the dark tale.

"No one was able to escape?" Paige asked, horrified. "It must have gone up very fast."

"That's just it," Luther frowned. "All the adults got out safely. Just none of the boys. It was very controversial at the time. Many people accused them of killing them on purpose."

"On purpose? That's horrible." Paige frowned too.

"Why would anyone think that adults would want to do that to young boys?" Nelson asked.

But it was Greg who jumped in. "Because! They were already under the control of the dark puppeteer!"

Paige gave him a look that said Don't-lead-the-witness, and he shrunk a bit in his chair. Nelson didn't argue though and even seemed to be weighing that possibility in his own mind.

"Well, I don't know about any puppeteer," Luther said, clearing his throat at the strange outburst, "but the boys were known troublemakers. They were from broken homes, poor homes where perhaps the parents couldn't afford to keep them, living on the streets, etc. These were not high-society boys."

"But to kill them? Or let them die horribly in a fire?" Paige asked astonished. Troubled boys might be challenging, but not deserving of a death sentence.

"Of course, there were tons of rumors and accusations in the court of public opinion, just as there would be if it happened today," Luther explained, "but no one was ever found to be guilty of anything. Just a senseless accident." He leaned on an elbow which he'd rested on the conference table. "The original building was completely lost to the fire. Nothing of it still remains, so the building of the 1920's you read about is unrelated to the boys' home."

"Yeah, but that doesn't mean there isn't a connection," Paige said, looking at Nelson.

Nelson wrinkled his brow in thought. They needed more. "Can you tell us the rumors and accusations? In our line of work those can be...quite compelling."

"Well..." Luther dragged the word out as if repeating such nonsense was beneath a man of scholarship.

Paige decided to level with him so he wouldn't stop helping. She'd found nothing out there in her brief research period about the Brethren Fire, so she was worried if Luther clammed up now, details might be difficult for them to find on their own. "I had a personal experience at the Olive last night. I was grabbed by what seemed to be a man—the puppeteer as we call him—" She spared a glance over at Greg who seemed pleased his name had stuck. "—and dragged to a hallway where I was surrounded by dozens of boys. We'll have evidence later I can share with you."

Luther's eyes widened again at the firsthand account.

"You *saw* ghost boys from the Brethren Fire?" Luther managed to stammer out.

Paige nodded and added, "So we need to know everything, no matter how trivial. We need to help put their spirits to rest."

Luther still had an expression of disbelief mixed with utter shock at the tale Paige had to tell, so Nelson added, "You'd be surprised how often a rumor turns out to be true enough to help us on a case."

Luther swallowed and then leaned in, like what he was about to say was utterly taboo and he'd be in trouble for saying it. "Well—" He looked around as if to make sure none of his colleagues were spying on him. "—there were rumors of the dark arts."

Greg laughed, but Paige simply asked, "Can you be more specific?"

Luther cleared his throat and stared at Greg. "I know it sounds ridiculous, but the townspeople of the time believed the boys were being mind-controlled by a warlock. With strange experiments and things happening to them at night when they were sleeping. Like they would wake up and not be able to breathe and such. And that the only way the adults could save them was to burn them before their souls were corrupted."

Greg slapped a hand on the table, "I knew it! A puppeteer." He was smiling, utterly proud of himself.

"It wouldn't be our first encounter with witchcraft," Paige continued, ignoring Greg's outburst yet again.

"It wouldn't be our first time with ridiculous either," Nelson added.

It was Paige's turn to lean in across the table that divided her from Luther. "Any clue who the warlock was? Or what he wanted with the boys?"

Luther shook his head. "Rumors only. Some said he was one of the adults that ran the reform school. Others thought he was some transient who visited the boys in secret. The most extreme thought he was always a dark spirit, controlling the boys from beyond the grave all along." Luther chuckled a bit at the last option, as if the very idea was complete nonsense.

But Paige and Nelson didn't consider it nonsense at all.

Paige turned to Nelson. "That could be possible, right? That the warlock—or puppeteer—" She nodded to Greg who beamed. "—was always a spirit?"

"Very. If every adult got out alive then they weren't missing anyone. So he was either always a spirit or he was one of the adults who escaped." Nelson nodded. "And you know as well as I that dark spirits can be very powerful."

"Would you happen to have a list of the adults who worked in the boys' school at the time of the fire?" Paige asked Luther.

Luther smiled in relief, happy to be back on

topics he felt comfortable discussing: real life history versus ghost stories and rumors. "Yes, of course. I'll print it for you." Luther got up and left the room.

Once he was gone, Greg stood up and began pacing. "I get it now. This is exciting. We're like Agatha Christie. All we have to do is figure out the puppeteer's identity and the mystery is solved!"

Paige grabbed his hand gently, but coaxed him back into his seat, treating him as a naïve child. "It's not always that simple."

Nelson added. "We don't know what he wants but some dark spirits use other souls to gain power. He may not give up the boys' souls so easily. And it might get worse before it gets better."

"Worse? But we already did the investigation, right? We tell the nightclub owner who is haunting his place and leave Seattle. Right?" Greg looked between Paige and Nelson. Nelson looked at Paige as if to say, 'He's your husband, you tell him.'

Paige sighed. "Honey. This is most likely very close to the beginning and nowhere near the end." She patted the seat next to her, again coaxing him to sit. This time he obliged, a look of concern plastered across his face.

"If we think we have a theory on who the puppeteer might be, then we'll go back tonight and test it out. And sometimes when confronted, dark spirits get....cranky." Nelson took off his glasses and cleaned them on his shirt.

"They get violent," Paige added.

"They can be nasty," Nelson nodded.

"I hate being scratched the most," Paige said.

"I hate being choked," Nelson announced as he placed his glasses back on his face.

"Scratched? Choked?" Greg asked, looking again between the two investigators. "Why on earth do you do this job?"

"If you stay 'til the end, you'll understand," Nelson said. Then he frowned and added, "At least, I think you will."

Paige placed a gentle hand on her husband's knee. "Those boys are victims. Garrett is a victim.

Even the puppeteer himself. Imagine being tormented or lost or sad for all eternity. Well, we help that. It's so much more than helping people. We're helping souls find peace. That feels important."

Before Greg could respond, Luther entered the room with a handful of papers in his hand.

"Here." He placed them in front of Paige. "This is the faculty." He pointed at a laundry list of names that sat under the title Brethren Reform School, and then turned to the next page. "And this is a photograph of them."

Paige gasped when she saw the old sepia, low-quality photo from the early days of the technology. But it didn't matter. The image was clear enough for her. "This is him. Doesn't this look like the shadow controlling those boys, Nelson?"

"Hmmm... Definitely some similarities. We can compare to footage when Duncan and Duane finish going through our evidence," Nelson said.

"Who is this man?" Paige asked Luther.

He leaned in and then checked the first page.

"That's Conan Henriksen. He was the headmaster."

"And he didn't die in the fire?" Paige asked skeptically.

"No. He was the one that helped make sure everyone got out." Luther responded.

"Everyone except the boys, that is?" Nelson asked, eyebrow up.

Luther seemed to mull that over in his mind. "Correct. Somehow he was able to get all the adults out, but none of the children."

Paige and Nelson exchanged another look. Maybe the unfortunate accidental Brethren Fire was no accident after all.

Chapter 6 – The Puppeteer in Your Nightmare

Duane was in the zone.

This was his favorite part of any investigation, and he was good at it. Headphones on, eyes on the screen, no detail too big or too small. A slight shadow shift? He grabbed it. A small orb floating across the lens? Captured. A voice, a creak, a whisper? Evidence.

He told himself it was because he loved watching the footage for evidence, and that was partially true, but he also really enjoyed the peacefulness of it. No one talking to him. No one expecting anything of him. Just him and hours of details that proved or disproved the supernatural.

They had been doing this long enough that often within a few minutes they knew without any equipment at all if a place was haunted. They could sense the energy shift in the air. The Olive Nightclub had been one of those places. Within minutes there was enough evidence to be confident this wasn't just a case of old pipes or drama queen clients.

He'd had footsteps, people being thrown and dragged, Paige's ghost children who appeared as dozens of bright heads on the footage, but it was what he'd heard in the background as they'd been packing up, considering the active night's investigation to be over, that had him excited. This was something new. Something none of them had known they'd captured.

"Duncan." He tapped Duncan's shoulder and removed his headphones. "Listen to this."

Duncan didn't love watching footage anywhere close to as much as Duane, and at least he wasn't as bad at it as Paige, but he wasn't all that great either. Sometimes Duane just wanted to say, "Let me do it all myself," but he knew that was rarely realistic with all the evidence that they typically captured.

Duncan took the headphones eagerly. He trusted Duane and he appreciated the break from the monotony of watching hours of footage.

Duane pressed play and Duncan listened to the gravelly deep voice say, "Let us burn." Duncan widened his eyes at the impressively clear enunciation. Most EVPs were garbled and tough to make out.

Duncan took off the headphones. "Do you know who that is?"

Duane shook his head.

"Is it the only clip?"

Duane shook his head again and rewound the footage to line it up with a different time stamp. Duncan placed the headphones back on his head and listened to the same gravelly voice say, "Who are you people?" Again, it was surprisingly articulate.

Duncan leaned in to see what was happening on the footage. Nelson was clearing equipment off the stage and Duncan could see his own large self in the foreground rolling up cables. "This is at the end of the night?"

"Yeah. When we were packing up."

Duncan ran his fingers through his long bangs. "He doesn't seem angry, but he wants to burn? Makes no sense."

"Especially in the context. Burning makes no sense. No one is burning or lighting any flames or anything. Perhaps it's a residual haunt?"

Duncan nodded. "Perhaps. But residual haunts caught on EVP and grabbing people are unusual. I'd like to hear Nelson's theory when he and Paige get back from the historian."

"And Greg," Duane added. He fought the urge to roll his eyes—for Paige's sake.

"Oh? Greg went too?" Duncan asked, truly shocked. He didn't think Greg had it in him to be this dedicated to the case.

"Yeah, I saw him leave with them this morning," Duane said as he cued the evidence back up to continue his work.

"Huh. Perhaps there's hope for him, after all," Duncan said.

At this Duane could not resist, and he did roll his eyes. "Doubt it. He's a sleepwalker."

"Sleepwalker? What do you mean?"

"That's what Celts call people who go through the motions in life. *Ceum-cadail*, that's the Celtic name for it. Wandering around, doing things without purpose, lost. Half-asleep their whole lives."

"Well, maybe Paige will help that. Her energy is infectious." Duncan put his headphones back on and Duane continued his focus as well, but he stole a quick thought of Paige helping Greg wake up to reality in his life. He supposed if anyone could, it'd be her. Sometimes her overly cheery self made him cringe, but he had to admit she *was* infectious.

They hadn't gotten very far when a vibrating in Duncan's pocket alerted him to the call coming through. A quick glance told him it was a call he wanted to take.

"Talk to me, Paige," Duncan answered.

"Have you captured any footage of the puppeteer?" Paige blurted out the instant she heard Duncan's voice.

"The puppeteer?"

"Oh. That's what we've been calling him. The

black shadow that controls the ghost boys," Paige explained.

"Yeah. We have tons of footage of that guy. Mostly from your little interaction under the stage," Duncan answered.

"I've got a photo to compare him to. I think it may have been the school headmaster." Paige filled Duncan in on what little they knew so far. They were driving back to the hotel, papers from Luther in hand.

"Ah. The old evil headmaster-slash-puppeteer situation." Duncan leaned his large frame back in the chair he was sitting in. He pressed a hand to his eye. Watching all the infrared footage in a dark room really strained the eyes.

"I'm serious, Duncan. I don't know what he was up to or after, or why he killed those boys, but I believe it was him," Paige argued.

"I believe you," Duncan said. "It just sounds like a bad plot to a television show or something."

Ignoring Duncan, Paige instructed, "Save the footage. We'll be there soon." And she hung up without a goodbye.

Duncan leaned in to Duane to catch him up to speed on all that Paige had told him, but Duane held up a hand. "No need. I'll hear it ten times before this case is closed."

Duncan nodded because he knew Duane was right, put the headphones back on and went back to reviewing the evidence. By the time Paige, Nelson and Greg had gotten back to the hotel room to join Duncan and Duane, they had gone through all the footage and voice recordings. They had gathered quite a collection for Garrett. Of course, Garrett had also been there so he'd seen many things firsthand, but it was always nice to hand a client proof that they weren't completely crazy.

That was what Duncan was used to hearing. *Just tell me I'm not crazy.* It was kind of funny to Duncan that people's first instinct to experiencing the paranormal was that there was something wrong with their brain. Is no one open to the idea anymore that it's because your brain is so *powerful* that you experience these things?

"Do you have footage of the puppeteer you can pull up easily?" Paige blurted out when she barged into Duncan's hotel room. Duncan had never been a very neat person—his disheveled look wasn't just for his clothes and hair. There was stuff everywhere, as if his suitcase and the investigating equipment had vomited all over his bed and furniture. Nobody really much cared, but suddenly Duncan became very aware of Greg's presence.

"Hi to you too, Paige," Duane muttered.

"I want to compare it to this," Paige extended the printout with the sepia-colored photograph of the school staff, waving it between Duncan's and Duane's noses.

Duncan and Duane exchanged a look but said nothing. Wordlessly, Duane cued up some of the evidence they'd captured to the spot where the dark shadow loomed ominously over the ghost boys. Paige cringed at the sight of herself on the screen reacting to the spirits all around her. When the puppeteer was at just the right angle, she pointed at the screen and shouted, "Right there. Pause it."

Duane did as instructed and then zoomed in on the dark shadowy figure they now called the puppeteer. His face was in shadow and what wasn't void of light was translucent. Distinct details were hard to see for certain.

"See?" Paige held the printout up near the screen as Greg and Nelson crowded in behind Duncan and Duane to judge for themselves. "Same build, same shape of the head, same nose..."

"Paige, I'm on board with your theory," Duncan said, "but there isn't enough to go on here to be conclusive. And even if there were, it just raises more questions. Why would the person most responsible for helping these boys kill them in a fire, escape with his own life, only to join them in the hereafter?"

Paige, deflated, frowned and let her shoulders slump. She'd been so excited about her certainty on who the black shadow was, that she got caught up in that and let it cloud her thinking.

But Nelson had her back and he jumped in to say, "Because he needed them dead."

Duncan shifted around in his chair, his weight forcing it to make strange creaking noises. "Go on."

"I think he could possibly be a mare. He would need souls to stay strong," Nelson explained.

"What's a mare? Like a female horse?" Greg had a strong look of disbelief plastered across his face.

"It's actually the basis for the word 'nightmare.' It's a demon that holds you down while you sleep and sucks your life force. Some people refer to it as sleep paralysis," Nelson explained calmly and rationally.

"Wouldn't it be easier for the headmaster to keep the boys alive and suck their souls at night in their sleep?" Duncan asked, curious about Nelson's theory.

Nelson shook his head. "My guess is, the mare only took the form to *look* like the headmaster. He was likely always an entity that was tormenting them. And torments them still."

"What from the case so far led you to this

conclusion?" Paige asked, a hint of skepticism lacing her words.

"Please don't set him off, Paige." Duane rolled his eyes, even though he remained facing the screens in front of him, hoodie up.

"Luther mentioned experiments on the boys while they slept, and that they would wake up unable to breathe and such." Nelson crossed his arms, as if that were enough to convince them all.

"But a mare? Why would you jump to a mythical creature before assuming a classic haunting?" Paige still argued.

Duane threw up his arms. "You did it. You set him off. Thanks, Paige."

"I've researched many cases on sleep paralysis and they all contain the exact same symptoms. Waking up to being very lucid, but unable to speak or move as you watch a dark shadow approach you, push on your chest until you can't breathe and suck your soul, while you lay frozen and unable to protect yourself. That's not a myth. That really happens to thousands of people all across the globe every year." Nelson nodded to punctuate his point.

Greg felt the need to stand by Nelson, both because he had no better theories and because Nelson had been welcoming to him from the start. "So how do we prove the theory that we're dealing with a mare?"

"We, Greg?" Duane still spoke without turning around. "You've spent all of one night investigating."

Paige slapped Duane's arm but Nelson answered Greg without reacting to Duane. He was used to him by now anyway. "I suggest two things. One is less...painful than the other. First, we need to research any sleep paralysis cases in, near, or around the boys' school or the nightclub." He looked at Paige, suggesting that she be the one to do the research.

Paige nodded. "I can do that."

Duncan raised an eyebrow, afraid to ask but knowing he needed to. "And the other?"

"One of us is going to have to go back to the nightclub...and go to sleep." Nelson looked around at all the faces staring back at him. No one volunteered immediately.

But after a few beats, Greg announced, "I'll do it."

Duncan took a deep breath. "No, it's okay. I'll do it. So I have a nightmare? Wouldn't be the first time on a case."

"Duncan." Greg stood up straight and even standing he wasn't much above a sitting Duncan. "I insist. I tagged along on this case and, as Duane pointed out, I haven't really proven myself just yet. Let me do this. To do my part."

Paige rubbed his arm, feeling very proud of him at this very moment.

Nelson turned to Greg. "You just have to sleep. If you are awakened to sleep paralysis, then we'll know we have our entity. We'll be filming and watching, so he won't be able to do much harm. But it won't be pleasant."

Greg nodded. He didn't relish the thought of waking up to not being able to move or breathe, but he also wasn't completely convinced it would even happen. He couldn't deny that he'd had some weird personal experiences in the nightclub, but a natural skepticism still filled his mind. A demon that sucks your soul while you sleep? *Yeah, right.*

"So let's say you're right, Nelson, and I know you usually are." Duane held up his hand as if to tell Nelson there was no need to explain further. "What does it even mean? How do we stop it? The only way I know to stop a nightmare is to wake up."

"Oh, mares are conjured, like most curses." Nelson shrugged. "We just have to counteract the conjuring."

"That doesn't seem so bad," Greg said.

Paige smiled at her husband. "Nelson has a tendency to gloss over the messy parts. Undoing a conjuring usually means a spell or a ceremony of some sort."

"Witchcraft?"

Duncan stepped in to clarify, "We prefer the term 'occult.'"

"We'll have to know who started the curse and

how. When we know that we know whether we are dealing with witchcraft or a religious ceremony of some sort," Nelson added.

"So whatever started the mare, we use to end it? Even if it's evil, too?" Greg asked.

Paige opened her mouth to justify their methods, but it was Duane who jumped in with a snort. "Everyone wants everything to be so black and white. But the reality is, sometimes the truth is a little murky and the only way to fight fire is with fire."

Paige smiled and added, "Can it really be evil if it's used to stop evil, Greg? We're the good guys here."

Greg nodded and said nothing. He wasn't convinced, but he knew he also didn't have much room for argument. As Duane said, he'd only been on one investigation.

Maybe he'd have more credibility after he'd experienced sleep paralysis.

Chapter 7 - Sleeping at The Olive

"Most of this evidence you witnessed firsthand, but at least you'll have it for your records," Duncan said as he sat across from Garrett at a small round table near the bar. The laptop was open and cued up. He played the footage and then the two new EVPs they hadn't heard real time, and Garrett watched, listened, and barely reacted.

"Well, I think we all know this place has something supernatural going on. The question is, could anyone get hurt? And how do I make it stop? I have a business to run." Garrett leaned back in his chair, his rocker-style hair swaying with the movement, arms folded across his chest.

It was closing time and Anthony was busy wiping down the bar and Miles was snoring at the back corner table. Minus Duncan's presence, it was so similar to the first night Garrett had witnessed the paranormal that it was almost eerie.

Duncan sighed. "You're not the first business owner to have financial concerns over ghosts. For homeowners it's usually emotional, but for business owners hauntings can be more...financially impactful."

Garrett ran a hand over his face before saying, "Do you actually know we have ghosts? I mean, is that truly what's going on here?"

"The spirits of the boys appear to be a very typical ghost-type haunting. We call those intelligent hauntings," Duncan explained.

"But..." Garrett strung the word out to encourage Duncan to finish the explanation.

"But the powerful dark entity that appeared to be controlling the boys—the puppeteer, we call him— he seems to be something...else."

Garrett widened his eyes but it was clear that this wasn't going to cut it for him. "Like what? How many types of ghosts can there be?"

Duncan chuckled. *If only they knew.* "Our

theory is that he's a mare. It's a conjured entity most commonly associated with sleep paralysis."

Garrett managed to be completely surprised by this news. "I thought that was proven to be just hallucinations. And no one who works here has had any sleep paralysis."

Duncan leaned back in his own chair, matching Garrett's posture, even if he was looming larger. "Well, the boys that lived here when this was a school apparently had incidents in their sleep. Or so we were told."

"It's not completely true." Anthony stopped cleaning the bar and yelled over to Garrett. "I had sleep paralysis."

"What? When? You never said anything," Garrett responded with a frown.

Anthony walked over to Duncan and Garrett at the table. "I didn't know it was anything worth mentioning. But it was a few months ago. I woke up in my room and I could see and hear fine, but I couldn't breathe or speak. And then a large shadow came over me and I felt a pressure on my chest, like something was sitting on me. Just as I started to panic a car alarm went off outside my window and everything stopped. The shadow, the pressure, the paralysis. All gone. I thought it was just a funky nightmare. But it was gawd-awful."

"Ah happen ta me too." Miles startled Duncan by coming up behind him silently, slurring his words.

Duncan twisted in his seat to face the ever-drunk patron. "You also had an experience with sleep paralysis?" Miles nodded. "Here in the nightclub?" He nodded again. "Well, I'll be…"

"I see even you had your doubts about that one." Garrett raised an eyebrow at Duncan.

"I have to admit, I thought it was a long shot."

"So what exactly does it mean?" Anthony asked.

"The mare feeds off the souls of its victims." Duncan didn't really want to meet Anthony's eyes as he explained that. "In their sleep or in their death."

"It was sucking my soul?! How did it get here?" Anthony asked.

Garrett leaned in and put a pointed finger down on the table between himself and Duncan. "And how do we make it go away?"

Duncan folded his arms across his chest. "Mares are conjured. It means someone summoned it here. We have to figure out who, what, where and why and then reverse the conjuring."

Garrett looked at Anthony, who shrugged in return. Garrett turned back to Duncan to ask, "Reverse it how?"

Duncan sighed. "I don't know yet. Could be a simple ceremony, could be more involved. We really won't know until we get to the bottom of it."

"And how do you do that?" Garrett asked.

"We're going to start by confirming we're dealing with a mare. From the experiences you guys have described, I now think it might be likely, but we'll have one of our own sleep here tonight and see if we can lure the mare to attack. And then, we'll ask it."

"Will it answer?" Anthony asked, wide-eyed.

"Maybe," Duncan answered cryptically.

Miles leaned his weight on the table with a drunken sway. "My wife."

"What?" Duncan asked, but Garrett waved Miles away.

"Pay no attention to him. He's just drunk."

"No." Miles couldn't focus his eyes, looking around the room at everyone and no one all at once. "My wife. Wuzzzz dare."

"I don't follow, sir. I'm sorry." Duncan shook his head.

"She saved meh." His head bobbled. "From sucking ma soul."

Duncan turned to Garrett. "Does his wife sometimes come here with him?"

Garrett frowned and his eyes softened. "She died many years ago."

"So, your wife's spirit protected you from the mare?" Duncan asked Miles, who nodded vigorously in return. "Sounds like you have quite the guardian angel."

"Does it work like that?" Garrett asked.

"I honestly don't know, but I believe that it can. Good spirits protect us from evil ones all the time." Duncan stood up. "I guess what I'm trying to say is, this case is just getting started. We have a lot more questions than answers right now. But here." Duncan removed a thumb drive from the laptop and handed it to Garrett. "This is yours. We start with proof of a haunting, which you have in your hands."

Garrett stood up as Duncan had. "We can be done here in ten minutes. Anthony and Miles, you guys head home. I want to stay." He looked at Duncan as if to make sure it was okay, and Duncan nodded in response. It was a bit unorthodox, but so was a mare in your nightclub disturbing the slumber of your employees and guests.

Anthony cleared his throat, putting his hands on his hips and looking at the ground. "I'm a little embarrassed to admit it, but I'm not sure I can sleep tonight now. Now that I know it was not just a bad dream."

"I'll have Paige bring you some sage. It wards

off spirit energy and should protect you," Duncan answered kindly. This wouldn't be the first young man to be afraid of a spirit—and even more afraid of how it made him seem. Anthony looked a bit skeptical at the spiritual remedy but didn't argue.

"When do we start?" Garrett asked Duncan.

"My team's on the way," Duncan answered.

By the time the Olive Nightclub was ready for the next day and Miles and Anthony were on their way home—Anthony with a bag of sage from Paige—the Paranormal Investigators League and Garrett and Greg were ready for the next test.

"We've slept on cots before," Duncan explained, showing Greg the makeshift bed they'd put together on the stage. "It won't make you forget your honeymoon suite, but hopefully it's late enough that you fall asleep regardless."

It was after three in the morning and Greg was definitely feeling the late hour, but he wasn't so sure sleeping on a stage with cameras pointing at him would allow him to just gently count sheep and relax.

Duncan pointed to the front of the Olive where the team was setting up equipment. "We'll be watching you the whole time, so you'll never be in danger. It probably won't be comfortable, though." Duncan frowned and Greg swallowed his nervousness.

Thudding footsteps alerted Duncan and Greg to someone coming up the stairs to the stage. They turned and saw Duane carrying a second cot. He placed it next to the makeshift bed for Greg.

"What's this about?" Greg couldn't help but ask.

Duane continued lining up the cot without meeting Greg's eyes. "I thought you might sleep better with Paige at your side."

"Where did you get a second cot?" Duncan asked. It hadn't been easy to procure the first one, and Duane just waltzed in with a second as if it were nothing.

Duane stood up and shrugged. "From my hotel room." His hoodie was up and covering his bald head.

"No. No way." Greg shook his head. "I don't want Paige here when this is happening."

"What don't you want Paige doing?" Paige came up to the edge of the stage and asked as she caught the sound of her name and the three men talking about her.

"Duane thought this might all go smoother if you were here with Greg. Help him sleep and such." Duncan raised an eyebrow. He really wasn't sure how she would feel about it and he planned to support her no matter what.

But Paige smiled. "Oh. Yeah, that's actually a good idea."

"I don't want any dark spirit sucking your soul," Greg explained a bit frantically.

Paige cocked her head to one side. "I'll just stay awake. Let me go get my pillow from the car."

"I don't like this," Greg mumbled, but he knew Paige well enough to know he wouldn't be talking her out of it tonight. And he was starting to just want to get it all over with.

"Paige is a professional," Duncan explained, trying to smooth the situation. "And she'll be right next to you if you need her. If the mare does attack, she can stop it from doing much harm."

"It can't hurt us both at once?" Greg asked.

"I don't think so," Duncan said. At least he hoped that was true. He didn't completely know, but he'd never heard of two people getting sleep paralysis at the same time in the same room.

By the time Paige bounced back into the room, Duncan, Duane, Nelson and Garrett were quietly sitting in the back of the room. They were used to late nights, but sitting in the quiet dark so Paige and Greg could sleep was already making Duncan's eyes a bit heavy. And they had no idea this would work anyway. Based on the experiences that Anthony and Miles had described, he felt more confident about Nelson's theory, but that still didn't give them much of a clue why the mare was here and how to stop it—if they could even prove it was a mare in the first place.

"It feels calmer tonight," Garrett leaned in to whisper to Duncan. "Do you think anything will even happen?"

Duncan shook his head. "No clue. But if this doesn't work, we'll regroup and try something else." He placed a hand on Garrett's shoulder. "We won't stop until we know how to make this end."

"I'm not worried about that." Garrett frowned, but his face still showed deep creases and worry lines. Perhaps he wasn't that eager to watch someone's soul be sucked from their body while they slept.

Duncan had seen a lot of weird things in his lifetime, but even *he* wasn't excited about people he knew facing a sleep demon.

The night was quiet, as Garrett had intimated, and the Olive was dark, as if the very shadows themselves had taken over the nightclub. Despite her proclamation to the contrary, Paige was the first to fall asleep while Greg continued tossing and turning in his little cot. They'd all essentially been awake all night, but Paige had seen quite the menagerie of paranormal entities in her time so she was just calmer than Greg when it came to what they were about to do. Greg had to tell himself it was no big deal—he was just going to sleep—but every time he closed his eyes he imagined the dark spirit from the investigation footage sucking his soul. The creepy thing had already dragged him across the room.

He listened to Paige's rhythmic breathing, allowing it to calm him. He even tried to match her pattern of breathing in, deep and slow, and exhaling, long and full.

It was no use.

He couldn't turn his brain off enough to fall asleep. So he added failure and frustration to the long list of emotions he was wrestling with staring into the dark ceiling above the stage.

And then he heard it. He assumed he heard it because he was listening to the silence so intently that the stark contrast from absence of sound to noise of any kind was jarring and noticeable. But most likely he would have heard it no matter what because it was there on the stage with him.

The rustling sound could have been anything— a rat or a small animal or something. It didn't mean it was paranormal. But he sat up anyway, resting on one elbow and peering across the stage into the darkness. Of course, he could see nothing.

But the sound was definitely there. And it was coming closer.

His senses were on high alert, peering intently into the shadows to see something—anything—that would match the sound. He saw nothing. He just heard a shuffling that was slowly coming toward him.

He didn't want to leave Paige, but he had to know what was making that noise. Without raising his voice above a loud whisper, he asked, "Duncan? Are you seeing anything?"

The rustling continued and Paige was as still as a stone next to him, still breathing rhythmically in deep sleep. His heart began pounding as the fear of the unknown mixed with the reality that *something* was in the dark and coming toward him and his new wife.

"We got nothing," Duncan responded, but his instinct kicked in and he began walking toward the stage. Despite his large strides, he only got about halfway before he stopped.

"Ohmigod," Greg yelled and scrambled off the cot, backing away from Paige who was lifting slowly off her cot. She kept rising until she was about three feet above where she'd been sleeping.

"Wake her up!" Duncan yelled at Greg as he began running toward the stage.

But Greg just stood there frozen in shock and fear at the sight of his levitating wife. As Duncan ran toward the stage, Paige began to gasp for air, making sucking sounds like she was breathing through a tiny straw and struggling to get any air.

Chapter 8 – Facing the Mare

"Wake up, Paige!" Duncan yanked on her, pulling her down from where she had been levitating above the cot. He cradled her in his arms as he shouted into the darkness, "Who are you? What do you want? And where did you come from?"

As Duncan yelled at the mare, seeing and hearing nothing in response, Greg grabbed Paige from Duncan's arms and confirmed that she was breathing again. She was. As she gained her bearings, she hugged Greg in relief that the whole thing was over.

"Man. That is frightening. Not being able to move while he steals your breath?" Paige shuddered, physically reacting to the horrible experience she'd just been through.

"Are you okay?" Greg asked frantically.

Paige nodded. "I'm okay."

Duncan took a glance at Paige sitting next to Greg and figured the worst was over. "Duane!" he called out. "Play back the video we just captured and see if we caught anything. Anything at all."

"Were you guys able to see it?" Paige asked.

"I couldn't see anything. Just hear it," Greg explained.

"Same," Duncan added. "I saw Greg sit up and you begin to levitate, but no mare or shadow or anything. You were just floating."

"I was?" Paige asked. At their affirmative nods, she added, "That explains it."

"No, Duncan. We don't see anything supernatural on the video," Duane shouted from the back of the nightclub.

"And no responses to my questions?" Duncan asked.

"Nothing."

"Rats!" Duncan muttered to himself. "So we don't know anything more than we knew earlier."

"That's not entirely true," Paige said, looking up

at Duncan.

"Oh?" Duncan raised an eyebrow in question and folded his arms. "Perhaps you should tell us what you experienced while you were levitating."

"It's just like they say. You can see and hear. You just can't move or breathe."

"That's awful, Paige." Greg squeezed her tighter, whether to comfort his wife or himself he was a bit on the fence about.

"You saw the mare? That no one else saw?" Duncan asked. He wasn't doubting so much as clarifying.

"Yes, and I heard him too. He crept over from the back of the stage wall, moving really slowly. Although I guess what need would he have to rush since I was paralyzed." Paige frowned at the memory.

"Interesting. So he showed himself to you and no one else as he sucked your soul." Duncan ran his fingers through his long, chestnut bangs as he so often did when he was piecing all the moving parts together.

Paige nodded. "He talked to me too. And he's

most definitely the headmaster. I saw him clear as day."

Nelson and Garrett approached the stage, although they stayed on the level where the patron tables were located. Only Duane remained in the back, eyes still glued to the screens, sitting low in a chair, hoodie up.

"What do you make of this, Nelson?" Duncan asked his well-educated teammate.

"I do think it's still possible he's just conjured to mimic the headmaster, but what kinds of things did he say to you, Paige?" Nelson responded, also pondering all the puzzle pieces.

"He said, 'Let them burn.'"

"That's what he said during the investigation," Garrett added.

"And clearly no one is burning anymore. I wonder if he's still referring to the dead boys," Duncan thought aloud.

"Duncan." With an unusually forceful tone, Paige forced his eyes down to where she still sat with

Greg. "There's more."

Duncan tightened his lips into a line before saying, "Why don't you tell us the whole story, Paige. Sounds like you had a wild, but not entirely fruitless experience tonight."

Paige stood and faced her team, her husband and their client. "I honestly didn't even know I'd fallen asleep, but I guess I had because I woke up to a scratching noise. I couldn't move or speak but I could see everything as if I were completely awake. I was fully conscious. That's when he stepped out of the shadows. Only there still were a bunch of shadows, so he must have been glowing or something. Anyway, I could see him clear as any of you standing here. He wasn't translucent or a shadow or anything. It was the headmaster. From the photo."

"I believe you. Go on," Duncan prodded.

"He crept toward me muttering some words, sounded like maybe an incantation." Paige looked all around her at the men who were listening intently to her story. "And when he got closer, he pulled me toward him—I guess that's when I levitated, but I didn't know. And then he looked straight into my eyes, no malice on his face, no anger or hatred, and said, 'Let them burn.' That's it. Then he stole my breath away. And I do mean that literally."

"And then we woke you up." Duncan nodded as he followed along.

"And he disappeared when you grabbed me, but, Duncan?" Paige looked up at her large boss. "When he talks about burning, I don't think he means the boys in the Brethren Fire. He was chanting. I think he means it as…a curse."

"So, what? Like, a fire he is planning?" Greg stood up and looked from Paige to Duncan.

"I guess we'd better do some research to find cases of sleep paralysis *and* fires in and around this nightclub over the years," Duncan said, folding his arms.

"Can we sleep first?" Duane's face remained impassive. "Paige is fine and we've been up for hours and now we're cursed to burn in a fire. Can we be done for the night?"

"I think we can wrap for now," Duncan agreed.

"It sounds like we have to hurry, though," Nelson added. "I don't know how much time we have between when the mare says the words and when the Olive burns down."

"*Burns down?*" Garrett shouted, the full gravity of what had just transpired hitting him in a wave of realization.

Nelson nodded. "So we'd better act fast."

Chapter 9 – Let It Burn

"I got a little sleep. I can start researching now," Paige told the team.

"Good idea, Paige. We can work in shifts," Duncan responded.

"I can do the first wave with Paige," Nelson answered, adjusting his glasses. "I'm used to all-nighters when I have a big project."

"Perfect. The rest of us will go get a little sleep and take the second shift," Duncan announced.

"Finally," Duane groaned.

Garrett bid them good night, although technically now it was merely an early morning, and headed home. The team parted ways in the hotel lobby and Nelson and Paige started with laptops in the breakfast dining area of the hotel. It was now late enough that there were a few people up and about starting their days. A slight drizzle was beginning to form outside and the streetlights gave it a soft glow. It was relaxing in its own way.

"I'll look for fires, you look for sleep paralysis," Paige instructed and Nelson didn't argue.

"Depending on what we find, we may have to go back to Luther," Nelson spoke as he frantically typed away in the search bar of his laptop.

"I know. I thought about that too." Paige entered her own search and then watched as the results populated the page. "Well, there are a lot of fires near the Olive,"

"I found a few reported cases of sleep paralysis, too," Nelson stated. "Do you have a map?"

Paige looked around. "No, but give me a minute and I'll buy one in the gift shop." She left Nelson reading about reported cases of sleep paralysis in the greater Seattle area. Many of them were college students just like Anthony. And they all said similar things to Paige: awake but unable to move as a shadow crept toward them. For some the spell broke quickly, but there were a few who felt what Paige had felt and had their breath sucked away. *What a horrible thing to wake up to.*

"Got it." Paige held up the map to show Nelson she had what he'd asked for.

"Let's plot all the fires and sleep paralysis cases we can find within six square blocks of the Olive," Nelson suggested.

"Why six blocks?" Paige asked, her short brown hair bouncing with the energy of cocking her head to one side.

Nelson shrugged. "It's somewhat arbitrary, but we can't assume every fire in Seattle is related to the mare. That's the boundary I chose."

Paige didn't argue. She was more curious than questioning the methods. "Okay." She dug in her bag and pulled out two pens, one for each of them. She kept the red pen, since that seemed appropriately symbolic for fires, and handed Nelson the black pen. As they read the articles for each of their stories they began circling landmarks and addresses where the events had occurred.

It hadn't taken very long for a pattern to emerge.

The fires were always located near where a reported case of sleep paralysis had occurred, and many times in the same location.

"Write down the date and time of the event if you have that information, too," Nelson instructed. Paige nodded in affirmation of the instruction. And again a pattern emerged. "The sleep paralysis always happens shortly before the fire."

"So the Olive is going to catch fire?" Paige asked.

"If we don't undo the conjuring first, it looks that way." Nelson adjusted his glasses.

"So how do we figure out who originally did the conjuring, and why?" Paige asked.

"How far back do the stories go that we've found so far?" Nelson asked, studying the map for the answer to his own question.

"I found a story back in the sixties," Paige

answered.

"And the Brethren Fire was 1896 Luther said, so what we need to do is figure out if that was the first, or just one of the many." Nelson gestured at the map to show the full picture of the destruction the mare had caused. There were ten black and red circles on the map already, but Paige took her red pen and circled one more to accentuate Nelson's point. She circled the Olive Nightclub.

"So you're thinking maybe the boys' school was just another victim and the mare started somewhere else?" Paige asked.

"It's just a theory," Nelson said, staring at the map. He circled the area near the University of Washington campus. "If there was another case or two prior to 1896 in this same vicinity, then maybe we are dealing with the aftermath in our current case, and not the start at all."

"But why would the mare look like the headmaster then?" Paige asked.

"Most people describe a shadow," Nelson

explained.   "You saw the headmaster but few saw anything close to the level of detail you saw."

Paige frowned. "What are you saying?"

"I'm simply saying we can't take it as anything more than one of many data points at the moment." Nelson squeezed her hand to let her know he believed her and didn't mean any disrespect.

"We gotta go. Now." The sound of Duncan's voice shocked both Paige and Nelson to the core.

"What's going on?" Paige asked as she studied Duncan's face for information. He looked upset and worried.

"There's a fire," Duncan stated, his mouth a tight line.

Nelson and Paige exchanged a look and then Nelson asked, "The Olive?"

But Duncan shook his head. "No. Anthony's apartment building."

Paige looked down at her map. They had forgotten to mark Anthony's sleep paralysis case, and now fire, on the map. Paige added one more circle to the map, making twelve total. Only the Olive hadn't also had a fire yet.

"What's this?" Duncan asked as he peered over their shoulders.

"We've marked every fire and sleep paralysis case we found within six blocks of the Olive," Paige explained.

"You can see there's a pattern. First someone gets sleep paralysis, then the building burns," Nelson explained.

Paige suddenly remembered the boys who had perished in the fire and she realized they had no idea if this was how the mare got its souls. "Is Anthony okay?"

"Yeah, he got out. He called Garrett and Garrett called me," Duncan explained, pulling back his long bangs with one hand. "Let's let Greg and Duane keep sleeping, but I think we should head on over."

"If we see the headmaster in the flames, I'm going to say 'I told you so,'" Paige said as she folded up the map and shoved it and the two pens back in her large shoulder bag.

Duncan looked questioningly at Nelson who simply stated, "Just a theory."

They drove as quickly as the wet roads and Duncan's old Chevy would allow. The flames were under control by the time they arrived, but thick, black smoke was still billowing up into the air, mixing as it did with the drizzle coming down. The P.I.L. team pulled up their hoods as they climbed out and looked around for Anthony.

He and Garrett were standing near a streetlamp that was still on from the night before. There were firefighters milling around and finishing up, their work here mostly completed as far as putting out the fire. A few smolders here and there were still popping up and needing to be put out, but the raging fire was, for all intents and purposes, over.

"Was anyone hurt?" Paige blurted out as soon as she came up to Anthony and Garrett. She knew it wasn't the warmest greeting, but her concern that the mare was using the fires to collect souls was overtaking her common courtesies.

Anthony shook his head. "I don't think so. Seems like the fire alarms did the trick. Everyone got out and the fire department got here quickly." He kicked a small rock with his shoe. "But looks like I'm going to be homeless for a bit while they repair the damage."

"You won't be homeless. It might not be easy, but this will all just be a story you tell one day," Duncan said, trying to cheer Anthony up.

"At least you were able to get out. I was worried about that," Paige said, her mouth fighting the frown that was threatening her face. Suddenly, something occurred to her, and she pulled out a paper from her oversized shoulder bag. "Did the entity that gave you sleep paralysis look anything like this?"

Anthony stared at the sepia-colored photograph of the headmaster before answering, "Maybe. I can't say for sure. He was more like a shadow, ya know?"

Paige pursed her lips and then quickly put the

photograph away before the drizzle in the air made it too damp or the ink started running.

"What does this all mean?" Garrett asked, his tone bordering on aggressive. Clearly this was all getting to him. "Is this related to the case at the Olive?"

Duncan looked at Nelson and Paige, and then decided they should share what they knew, even though it wasn't much yet. Duncan had always preferred to be open and honest with clients anyway. It wasn't always easy, but everyone just wanted to know what was going on. And no one liked being coddled. Especially when their lives and livelihoods were on the line.

He gestured with his head to indicate they should fill Garrett in.

Nelson leaned in. "We don't know for sure, but it seems to be related to the mare, yes. There have been a dozen sleep paralysis cases in this neighborhood over the past century or so, and *all* those cases have preceded a fire."

Garrett looked at Anthony, who was still

watching the small rock at his feet. There was something about the rock that was more important for Anthony's attention right now than worrying about how he almost died and how he wasn't sure where he would live. Garrett then looked up at the building, now no longer on fire, but still smoking with the residue of the events of the morning.

Still staring up at the building he asked, "So what exactly are you saying?"

Nelson knew Garrett was a smart man and most likely understood the implications of all that Nelson was saying, but he decided to say it anyway. He decided that it would help all of them process it and understand what they were dealing with to the full extent if he simply put it out there in words. Thoughts and concepts were easy to avoid and hide from, but words could make something real. They had the power to turn dreams into reality with their sheer weight. And sometimes you needed to hear to completely understand the thoughts that couldn't quite form inside your own head.

Nelson placed his hands on his hips. "I'm saying that every case of sleep paralysis has been followed by a fire. Every time. Which means...if we don't stop the mare soon, the Olive Nightclub is the next to catch fire."

Chapter 10 – The Past

"Was the Brethren Fire first? That's what we need to know." Duncan sat in the coffee shop of the hotel with his team and Greg. They had managed to get in a few hours of sleep after the long night investigating and researching. And now, the following afternoon, with their body clocks nice and off kilter, they knew they had to get to the bottom of their latest case. "If we know where the first incident happened, we can narrow down who conjured the mare."

"I also did some calculations," Nelson explained, leaning forward with his elbows on his knees. "There's a cadence to the events. A regular cadence."

"Meaning they're all regularly spaced out?" Duncan asked.

Paige jumped in to elaborate on Nelson's

findings. "There is a strong pattern between cases. They start out decades apart but slowly get closer together, as in the case with Anthony's apartment and the Olive."

"So what does that tell us?" Duncan asked, his hands folded on his head and pinning back his long bangs.

"It tells us," Nelson answered, "that the Brethren Fire was most decidedly *not* first. Based on the pattern, it was second, and the first happened twenty years prior."

"So we're talking 1876," Paige explained to the team.

"Okay. So we're looking for a fire near where the Olive is now in 1876?" Duncan asked.

Paige looked around her team. She was hesitant to say what was on her mind because she felt like she might be getting too myopic in her viewpoint, that maybe she was becoming obsessed and it was clouding her judgment. But she had to say it anyway. It just felt too important. "I want to research where the headmaster was in 1876. I just feel like he's connected somehow."

Duncan nodded. "Sometimes in this business, trusting your instincts is all you have."

"And I'll look for fires coinciding with sleep paralysis circa 1876," Nelson added.

"You may have to go back to the historian for that one. It sounds obscure," Duncan mentioned, and Nelson nodded in response. He'd been prepared for that eventuality.

"I'll go with Nelson. I'm curious about the origins, too," Greg announced. Paige smiled with pride and Duncan nodded, clearly impressed. Greg was starting to become one of them despite his initial skepticism. Firsthand experiences will often do that to you. Duncan knew that it was easy to be a non-believer when you just go through an ordinary life, but the shield of disbelief is easy armor to crack once you've encountered the supernatural with your own senses.

Like watching your wife levitate.

"And what exactly do you want me to do?" Duane muttered. He barely looked like he was awake, leaning back in his seat, hands in his pockets, hoodie up hiding the Celtic cross tattoo that covered the back of his bald head.

"You and I are going to go back through the footage from when Paige was sleep paralyzed and see if we can find any clues we missed," Duncan stated. Duane seemed to be pleased with that and he grunted in return.

"Do we know that the fires are tied to the location and not the people?" Paige asked, wide-eyed. It had popped into her brain that perhaps it was she who would burn and not the Olive, since she was the one the mare had confronted.

"You know the locations do coincide. You saw it on the map." Nelson frowned. "But no, we don't know for sure if the curse is to the person or the location."

"Why don't you add that to your list of things to research, Paige? Find out everything you can about mares, their summonings and how those curses work," Duncan instructed. Paige swallowed hard. She wanted to know. She *had* to know. And yet, the prospect was daunting at the very least.

Nelson stood up. "Ready, Greg? We're on a clock."

Greg stood and rubbed his hands together in anticipation. "Let's go." He kissed Paige on the cheek and he and Nelson left the team, everyone with separate marching orders.

The drive to Lake Union in the P.I.L van was pleasant. Greg was finding that he really liked Nelson. They chatted comfortably about life, and the case, and Paige. The time passed easily and they again pulled up to the fancy historical society building that was oxymoronically very modern.

Luther again met them at the front to welcome them.

"We need all the fires in Seattle in 1876," Nelson jumped in with no preamble.

Luther reacted in surprise. "1876 now? Your

haunting wasn't related to the Brethren Fire?"

"It is actually," Greg answered.

"It just wasn't the first," Nelson added.

"Wasn't the first what? There are many interconnected fires in the 1800's?" Luther asked with an air of skepticism.

"Not fires. Mares." Greg explained.

"Sleep demons, or more commonly known as sleep paralysis," Nelson explained.

Luther shook his head. "I'm sorry. Sleep demons? What does that have to do with the Brethren Fire?"

"Someone conjured a mare, or sleep demon, in 1876. Based on the pattern of sleep paralysis followed by fire, the Brethren Fire was the site of the second incident, not the first," Nelson explained.

"So we need those 1876 fires, please," Greg added. "Before the next fire."

Luther wrinkled his brow in confusion, but thankfully asked no further questions. He led them to the meeting room and left to gather the information they requested.

"Do you think this is the first time he's been asked about the history of sleep paralysis?" Greg asked.

"Undoubtedly," Nelson stated. "Which is surprising, given there's a pattern. Humans love patterns. You'd have thought by now someone would have questioned the pattern."

"But most people think sleep paralysis is just a dream state. I searched it online. All the articles say when you experience it, you're just half asleep. So no one would have assumed the fires were part of a demon conjuring."

"It's interesting to me that as a scientist I always told myself to be completely open-minded to all the possibilities. That's how I ended up studying paranormal phenomena in the first place. But so many scientists *want* the answer to be mundane and therefore force the data to say what they want it to be, instead of what it is or is a part of."

"So you don't think there is any validity to it just being a dream state?" Greg asked.

"That could definitely be true some of the time. Or maybe it's true all of the time, but the demon being present is also true. Both things can be true and not negate the other," Nelson explained.

Greg nodded and weighed the concept over in his mind. The more he experienced the supernatural, the more he realized that maybe sometimes people just didn't want to believe—himself included. But he couldn't deny his experiences. He had no way of explaining them rationally or scientifically, but he knew they were real.

Of course, the Paranormal Investigators League had captured tons of evidence during their cases. They had a prolific YouTube channel that was quite popular. But he already knew when they posted the evidence from this case, half the people would call it a hoax and accuse them of using special effects.

Heck, he had been one of those people a week ago.

But he knew what he'd experienced now. *Something* had happened to Paige, and it wasn't natural, or simply a dream state. He'd never heard of someone being able to levitate just because they were dreaming.

"There were four fires in 1876," Luther announced as he walked back in the room. "I think based on location, we can narrow it down to two that might be related to the Brethren Fire."

He placed a paper in front of Nelson and Greg and showed the two dates and addresses. To compare to what they'd already discovered, Nelson pulled out the map that Paige had purchased earlier that morning and on which they had taken notes on dates and locations.

"Can you circle the locations on this map for me?" Nelson asked Luther.

"Of course," Luther grabbed a pen from the conference table and used his left index finger to pinpoint the two addresses. They were both only just around the corner from the reform school that had burned in 1896.

"Anything significant to note with either of

these locations or the fires themselves?" Nelson asked.

"Not really. To tell you the truth, I didn't even know there had been four fires in 1876 until today." Luther traced his fingers over the circles and notes that had already been on the map. "1896, 1906, 1916, 1921, 1921, 1941, 1951, 1961, 1966, 1966, 1986, 1996, 2016... The pattern keeps starting over."

"Yes. And all these fires were also correlated with someone in the location claiming to have experienced sleep paralysis," Nelson explained. "So the next question is, of these two locations in 1876, did anyone claim to experience sleep paralysis before the fire happened?"

"I can look that up, but..." Luther looked at Nelson and Greg uncomfortably.

"Yes?" Nelson encouraged.

"Well, it might not be related but based on what you've discovered... There was a woman who died in this fire—" Luther pointed at one location on the map. "—who was documented as a witch. Witch-hunting was much rarer by 1876, but certainly people still believed in it in strong Christian communities."

"Can you share with us everything you know about her?" Nelson asked.

"Give me a sec." Luther left and came back within a few minutes with a laptop. He pulled it open and showed them an entry from his digital archives. "This is her. One of the only historical documents about witchcraft in this neck of the woods. That's why I remembered it."

Nelson's eyes widened. "Dolly Henriksen. Isn't that the same last name as the headmaster from the reform school?"

Luther frowned and then entered a search. "Oh, yeah. Conan Henriksen. You have a good memory."

Greg and Nelson exchanged a look and then Nelson leaned in and said, "We need to know how those two are connected."

Luther went back to the Dolly Henriksen entry and scanned for personal documents. There was a marriage certificate to a Reginald Henriksen. "So she married into this family. Perhaps Reginald and Conan were related. Give me a minute." Luther entered more search terms and an 1850 census listed Reginald and Conan in the same household. "They were brothers."

"Brothers." Nelson repeated.

"So what does that mean, exactly?" Greg asked.

"I don't know for sure who summoned the mare, but this gives me great confidence on the location of the first visitation," Nelson stated. He folded his arms across his chest with the finality that a major milestone had just been reached. "And who his first victim was."

"So, she was a witch but became the victim of a conjuring? I know I'm new at all this, but doesn't that seem backward?" Greg asked.

Nelson waved off the question. "You can't put too much weight on people's accusations. They were based on nothingness sometimes. But out of curiosity," Nelson leaned in to Luther to ask, "what evidence did they have against Dolly Henriksen?"

"Here's the full article. I can print you a copy."

Luther turned the laptop toward Greg and Nelson to show an electronic scan of an old-style newspaper article. "Essentially, she confessed to witchcraft after her neighbors accused her of causing a rain-induced flood. When the authorities investigated, they found quite a pile of grimoires and books on the occult and spiritualism. She later recanted, but it was too late by then. Everyone knew her as a witch."

"They based their theory on rain? In Seattle?" Nelson asked.

"So, she wasn't actually a witch?" Greg asked, trying to keep up as things came to light.

"According to the court documents, she was," Luther explained.

"I think we'll need to find out who owned those spellbooks. A lying witch is nothing new, but what if she was telling the truth when she recanted and someone planted those books to frame her?" Nelson was thinking out loud.

"So, you're thinking maybe one of the Henriksen brothers?" Greg asked.

"Unless they were victims too," Nelson said. He turned to Luther. "Were there any other rumors of witchcraft? And did the Henriksen family have any known enemies?"

Luther shook his head. "The biggest villain in this story, as far as history is concerned, is Dolly herself."

"What about other family? Relatives? Children, perhaps?"

"Umm." Luther typed into his laptop and scanned for the information he was seeking. "No known children for Conan, but Dolly and Reginald had one son. He was a teenager when his mother died in the fire. His name was Joseph."

"Any headlines associated with Joseph Henriksen?" Nelson asked.

Luther spent some more time searching, reading, typing on his laptop before finally shaking his head. "Doesn't seem to be. Sounds like he lived a quiet life. Got married, started a family, worked as a farmer, died in his fifties, so fairly young. But certainly no evidence that he was cursed or did any cursing. And other than the fire that killed his mother, no fires around him either."

Nelson rubbed his chin as he ran over the latest information.

Greg watched him and struggled to figure out who could have possibly conjured the mare. "What are you thinking, Nelson?"

"Well, I'm thinking that Paige is convinced the mare is Conan Henriksen and the first victim is Dolly Henriksen, so the conjuring is centered around these two somehow," Nelson responded. "One of them is the curser or they are both victims of the curse. Let me call Paige and see if she discovered anything while she was researching."

He had barely typed in her number and let the phone ring once when Paige answered, her voice breathless with the excitement that only Paige could muster during an investigation. "Nelson! I knew it. I knew it was the headmaster."

Nelson gave a questioning side eye to Greg,

although he had no idea what it was all about since Nelson was the one talking to Paige. "Oh? What did you stumble upon?"

"I found an anthology all about the international lore of sleep demons and mare curses. The Henriksen family name is all over this thing," Paige explained. Then suddenly she realized Nelson had called her and he must've had a reason. "Why? What did you find out?"

Still making eye contact with Greg, Nelson answered, "The first fire killed a known witch named Dolly Henriksen. She was the headmaster's sister-in-law."

"That bastard," Paige expressed her feelings out loud. "He kills an innocent woman and the children he was supposed to protect?"

"We don't know for sure she was all that innocent. She was a convicted witch."

"What could she have possibly done that deserved to have her soul sucked from her body as she slept just before she was burned to death?" Paige said skeptically. She was still convinced that it was all Conan Henriksen, but Nelson was less so.

"What if Conan was a victim too?" Nelson asked, exploring possibilities.

"Meaning?" Paige asked while Greg just watched Nelson's one-sided conversation, eager for it all to make sense.

"There is one person that ties them together. Perhaps we need to find out more about Reginald Henriksen."

Paige sighed at Nelson's logic. "Fine. Meanwhile, I'll borrow this anthology from the library. It's filled with spells and counter spells so we can end this thing before I burn to death like Dolly."

"We won't let you burn to death, Paige," Nelson responded.

"Mares need souls. One way or another, it's going to take one. And soon. You know this, Nelson," Paige explained.

"Not if we send it back to Hell first," Nelson answered. "See you back at the hotel in a bit." He ended the call and turned to Greg. "Paige found a very useful book for ending the curse. Now we just need to know who started it."

"How are we going to find out?" Greg asked.

"Like any good mystery, you start with the person who had the most to gain." Nelson turned to Luther, who was still sitting there in front of his laptop. "Give me everything you've got on Reginald Henriksen."

Chapter 11 – The Curse

Garrett sat across from Duncan in the dimly lit Olive Nightclub. Garrett knew he'd have to open his doors soon, but he needed to know some details before he could. The last thing he wanted was to open his doors and then have a fire destroy everything, including the lives of his patrons.

At a table next to Garrett and Duncan, Paige, Nelson, Greg and Duane sat watching and ready to jump in with information as needed. They were happy to let Duncan do most of the talking.

Anthony stood at the bar, ready for his shift, but also heavily vested in the conversation Duncan and Garrett were having. He wiped down the counter and set up the barware, giving his hands something to do while he listened.

"Duane and I watched the footage over and

over. We've come to the conclusion that the dark entity controlling the souls of the boys here in your bar is not the same entity as the mare. While Paige was having her encounter, we were able to see the dark spirit watching in the corner."

"Oh, God. So we have how many entities and a mare? This is ridiculous." Garrett threw his hands up in exasperation. It felt like every time they learned something new, there were more hauntings happening at his nightclub.

"We were also able to find out why the dark entity looks so much like the mare. They were brothers," Duncan continued.

"So you know who started the curse?" Garrett asked, a hopefulness brimming in his eyes for the first time in weeks.

"We do," Duncan nodded. "The Henriksen family has a long, dark history entwined with alchemy and the dark arts. They certainly would have known all they needed to know to summon a mare. Two brothers, Reginald and Conan, moved to Seattle from the East Coast. Reginald got married and settled down, but Conan never got married." Duncan paused and leaned in. "Because he was in love with his brother's wife."

Paige couldn't contain it any longer and she stood up to continue the narration where Duncan had left off. "In our line of business, gossip can be more useful than historical documents and we found an old gossip column that insinuated that Dolly's and Reginald's son, Joseph, may have actually been Conan's. Anger at his wife and brother could certainly prove motive enough to a man with Reginald's talents."

"So first he punished his wife by having her take the blame for a flood that caused a lot of damage. Framed her by planting *his* grimoires in her room so she looked like a witch," Duncan added.

Garrett shook his head. "Jealousy is a bitch, man."

"Well, jealousy and lust for power. A truly deadly combination," Nelson added. "The mare wasn't just about punishment. Even in death, when the mare takes a soul, Reginald's spirit becomes more powerful. And when he needs more souls, the cycle begins again. That's why you probably had no real experiences up until recently.   He was living a powerful afterlife separate from the physical world. But when it was time for more souls, he had to come back."

"But I don't get it. Can't he just eat all those boys' souls or something? He has dozens of them," Garrett asked.

"To fully recharge, the mare needs living souls. And we believe this is where the punishment for Conan comes in. See, Dolly got off kind of easy. He just sacrificed her to the sleep demon. She perished in the fire, energized the demon, and her soul crossed over. Or at least we don't see her presence anywhere. But Conan." Duncan wagged a finger. "Conan is the very crux of the curse."

Garrett looked at Anthony, who shrugged, before asking, "So what exactly does that mean?"

Paige shook the book of the occult she had found and was holding in her hand as she spoke. "The summoning spell is in this book. Reginald murdered his brother, sacrificing him and selling his soul. He made Conan into a sleep demon."

"Whoa," was all Anthony could say.

"But how could he have been the sleep demon when he was able to escape the Brethren Fire?" Garrett asked.

"It wasn't Conan that day. It was Reginald." Nelson stood up to match Paige. "In the historical records, Reginald disappeared without a trace the day of the first fire in 1876. But only one body was found that day. Dolly's. But Conan, who had up until that point lived a very quiet life, was suddenly very active in the community."

"One of the brothers killed the other. We know that based on the spell. And it's easy to see how they could be confused. Reginald just pretended to be Conan, essentially faking his own death in the process. They look so much alike." Duncan waved to Nelson. "Show Garrett the photos."

"Oh, yeah." Nelson dug through a pile of papers

he had stacked on the table and held up a printout of a very old looking photograph of two men, a young lady and a young boy. "Reginald, Conan, Dolly and Joseph. A very twisted family."

From under his black hoodie, Duane muttered, "Everyone always thinks their family is the most screwed up. But in this case, I think they were right."

Garrett grabbed the printout and studied the two men. Same jaw line, same haircut, same tight-lipped expression. "They do look a lot alike."

"That's why I kept thinking the puppeteer was the headmaster." Paige spared a glance at Greg, who smiled at the perpetuation of his original moniker. Even if this was his only significant contribution to the case, he was proud of it. "They're brothers who look so much alike."

"Okay." Garrett placed the paper back on the table in front of himself and looked the investigators head on. "Let's say I believe you about all this revenge-cursing-sleep-demon stuff. What do we do about it?"

Duncan cleared his throat. "Um…we're going to

have to trap the mare."

"Meaning someone goes to sleep again?" Garrett looked Duncan straight in the eye. "No. No way. That did not turn out well the last time we tried it, and now my place is destined to burn."

"Last time we didn't have this." Paige smiled as she held up the book she'd found. "And when the mare says to let them burn, he does mean both. The curse is on both the human—*me*—and the location. So we're in this together now."

"But Anthony didn't burn." Garrett pointed at his young employee, who startled at the mention.

"He's here, isn't he? We don't know that the mare is done with him," Nelson explained, and Paige shot him a look that said handle-more-delicately-next-time.

But Anthony puffed his chest out and spoke up for the first time since the P.I.L team had arrived. "Paige is right. Me. Her. Another group of schoolchildren. If we don't stop it, there will be another victim. We need to end this."

Garrett sighed. "Fine. We trap the mare. Then what?"

"Then we trap the puppeteer and we send both brothers back to Hell where they came from," Duncan said, leaning back in the chair he dwarfed, arms folded across his chest.

Garrett huffed a humorous laugh and stood up. "You make it sound so easy."

"Shall we get started?" Duncan asked, standing up also.

Garrett shrugged. "How much time do we have before we burn?"

Duncan looked at Nelson who shook his head. "We truly don't know."

"Then it doesn't sound like it's worth the risk of waiting. I've got a business to run," Garrett responded. "Let's do this."

Anthony came over to the group. "Once the mare is gone, what happens to the young boys who are trapped here?" His forehead was creased and it was easy to see he felt a kindred spirit with those young boys who just a short time ago had terrified him. The bony hand had been the original catalyst for calling the investigators. But now, they were victims just like he was.

Paige walked over to the young college student and placed a gentle hand on his forearm. "Once the puppeteer is gone, they'll be free and we can help them cross over. They'll finally get to be with their families in Heaven."

"Depending on how this goes, Garrett, you may have to close the Olive for the night," Duncan said pragmatically to their client. He didn't want to let Garrett believe this could all be over in fifteen minutes. It might—or it might be another really long night.

Garrett nodded in understanding. "So be it. I'd rather close one more night than keep living with the possibility that my place could burn down or Miles drinks too much and gets haunted by a demon that wants to suck his soul. I'm ready to do whatever's in that book." He gestured at the book Paige still held onto. Anthony stood next to her with his eyes widened at the prospect that lay ahead. Then Garrett added, "You don't have to stay, Anthony. I can call you if we end up opening."

"I'm not really eager to face all this again, but I'm not leaving," Anthony said, swallowing. "I'm seeing this through. For myself. For Paige. And for those young boys."

Duncan clapped his hands together. "All right. With that settled, let's get ready to summon and then trap the mare."

"Set it up on the stage, Duane," Paige instructed, as she thumbed through the book to find the right spell.

Wordlessly, Duane responded by walking over to Paige and holding out his hand. Rolling her eyes, Paige handed the book over to her fellow investigator. He scanned the pages for the full list of things required, grunted, and then handed the book back to Paige.

The black duffel bag that contained many of their candles, spices, and other spell necessities was sitting on the floor next to the nightclub table where

Duane had been sitting. He picked it up, letting the items inside the bag jingle and jangle as they moved around from being transported, and carried it to the stage.

The lighting in the nightclub was often a soft glow, an evening ambience. But the stage was completely dark, so Duane flipped the switch before dropping the duffel bag and let a flood of light spill across the stage floor. After rummaging around in the bag, he pulled out a piece of white chalk and began drawing symbols on the floor, all connected by a line that made a large eight-pointed star. At each point he placed a candle. He pulled out the crucible that he often used for combining ingredients for various ceremonies. Then he dug around and found small jars of what looked like everyday spices.

Greg walked over to Paige and whispered, "How does he know how to do all this?" Greg was no longer as skeptical of using spells and witchcraft as he was curious about what he was watching. Just as they'd predicted, they'd ended up using witchcraft to battle witchcraft. It wasn't his favorite pastime, but he was beginning to understand the methods.

After all, *he* wasn't the one setting up a ritual of the dark arts.

"Duane is experienced in Celtic ceremonies, which are pagan like witchcraft and the occult. They both use natural energies and elements of the earth to generate their power. Any one of us could follow the spellbook," Paige said and shrugged, "but Duane just does it so naturally none of us ever question it anymore."

"Will this…" Greg struggled to find the words of what he was asking. "Will this protect you from burning?"

Paige frowned. The reality of their job was sometimes it got dark before it got lighter. They had to face some evil horrifying things, even at the risk of their own peril at times. She'd never worried about it before. It just was what it was. A side effect of the job. But now, looking at Greg's concern plastered all across his face, she realized her life wasn't just her own anymore. She'd made a commitment to share her life with this man and that meant the risks were shared too.

She looked over at Duncan, who was busily setting up cameras and focusing the shot where Duane was setting up the spell. She knew he'd let many things go by the wayside to continue doing this job, including relationships.

Was it just so hard to be married and hunt ghosts and the supernatural?

So, she thought to herself, what would Duncan do? And she knew immediately. The only way to make this work was to be honest. Duncan always said that people want the truth. They want answers. They don't want to be shielded from the reality that they can already sense around them.

"I don't honestly know. There's still a risk to myself and Anthony," Paige explained. There was caution in her eyes, but she was determined to level with her husband. "But if we hurry and we do this right, then the curse is over and no one else has to get hurt by the mare. Ever again."

He didn't really know what to say in response, so he put an arm around Paige's shoulder and pulled her close. "Where you go, I go."

"Just focus on the spell and everything will be fine."

"I don't know anything about witchcraft."

"If you stick with us, this'll be your first, but not your last."

Greg turned to Paige with a raised eyebrow. "How often do you use witchcraft?"

Paige smiled, her usual bouncy self back on full display. "Whenever the occasion calls for it." She walked over to the edge of the stage. "How much longer, Duane?"

"Never rush an artist," Duane muttered in response. The stage did look ready for a spell. The markings looked like symbols and strange letters from a foreign language and by now, they completely covered the stage.   There were tealight candles covering the edges of the markings—Paige estimated another twenty in addition to the ones Duane had placed at the peak of each star. She was impressed they'd had that many in the duffel bag.

Paige swallowed hard before asking, "Do we have to use fire? Is there no other way?" She couldn't help it. Her mind kept playing scenarios of all the things that could go up in flames from a stage covered in candles.

Duane turned to her, his face aglow from the shadow of his black hoodie and the candles lit up beneath him. "Earth, wind and fire, little Paige. You know the drill." And then with no softness in his expression he added, "I won't let anything happen to you." And he turned back to his work.

It was possibly the nicest thing Duane had ever uttered to her and, oddly enough, it did provide some comfort. She began to shake her right hand nervously, both with eagerness to get everything underway and with the anticipation of what lay ahead.

She was nervous about the candles. She didn't feel like burning tonight.

Nelson came up behind her and placed a hand on her shoulder. "Turn to the right page in the spellbook. We need to get in place."

Paige began to comply even as she answered, "Duane is still setting up."

"I know, but I don't want to waste a single second when he's ready." Even Nelson was nervous. Everyone was nervous.

And, as if he had sensed something impending, the ground began to shake violently beneath their feet. Paige looked up at Nelson, who returned her look of fear.

They were out of time.

"Reginald knows what we're up to. He knows this spell. We've got to get started. Now!" The usually calm Nelson shouted the order and those who weren't on the stage already jumped up there quickly.

Duncan pressed *record* and joined them.

The shaking continued, which forced a candle to slide toward Paige and catch a flame on her pant leg. Greg ran to her as her pants went up in flames.

Nelson took the spellbook out of her hands just before she fell on her bottom, still struggling to put out the fire already beginning to engulf her.

"Let them burn," a voice echoed all around them.

Chapter 12 – Let Them Burn

"Duane!   Now!" Duncan instructed as he watched Paige and Greg both frantically slap the flames climbing up her pant leg. They would sometimes smother it for a second or two, but then it would suddenly burst back into flame, continuing to engulf her pant leg as violently as before.

"Why can't we put the flames out?" Greg asked anyone and no one.

From experience, the team knew the only way to help her was to do what they came to do. And quickly. Without hesitation, Nelson tossed the spellbook to Duane. Duane turned to the spell Paige had marked and began reciting.

Duncan walked over to Paige and extended a hand. "Because you can't put them out that way." Paige's eyes still reflected sheer panic at the situation she was in—the very one she'd most feared—but she steeled herself anyway and stood up, burning pants and all.

"Get in a circle!" Duncan instructed everyone, most of whom were standing around watching Paige's flaming pants in horror. Anthony was almost shaking, knowing that one false move and his fate could be the same. But they complied, although their circle was clumped and haphazard. "Everyone find a symbol Duane has drawn on the stage and stand in front of it!"

Thankful to have explicit instructions, Garrett ran to a crescent moon. Anthony found a symbol that looked like a planet with two rings. Nelson stood near an upside-down triangle with a line through it. Duncan grabbed the one closest to him, which reminded him of the infinity symbol if it were looking in a funhouse mirror. Paige hobbled over to a circle with three arrows. Only Greg could stand in complete shock where he'd already been, the urge to keep slapping Paige's pants leg, useless as it may have been, still overtaking him.

"What do we do now?" Garrett shouted across the stage.

"Arms out. Like this," Duncan shouted back, extending his arms as if he were about to give someone a hug. They copied him, Paige closing her eyes and wincing from the heat searing up her legs. She took deep soothing breaths to try and ignore the heat and pain and avoid panic. It was barely working.

Duane finished some passage and then shouted over his shoulder, "Repeat this part after me: *Trapiwch y cythraul cysgu!*"

Stumbling over the strange words, they repeated as best they could. Duane shouted, "Again! *Trapiwch y cythraul cysgu!*" A loud moaning sound echoed through the air above their heads, an eerie soundtrack to their spell. But, soft as it may have been, Paige thought she also heard the sound of laughter, as if the puppeteer were mocking their meager attempt to subdue him. They repeated the spell again.

"Keep saying it until we see the mare," Duane explained to the team. In a chanting way, they began to repeat the words over and over. The moaning continued, and so did the flames burning Paige's pants. Her entire right leg was covered in flames. She was breathing heavily but continued chanting. She knew it was the only way to end the torture.

They had repeated the spell Duane taught them a dozen times when a dark shadow figure appeared in the center of the stage. Garrett gasped and took a step back, but Duane answered, "Don't worry. He's spellbound. He can't hurt you."

Paige covered her mouth with her hands at the sight of the mare who had sucked her soul in her sleep just a few nights prior. He wore a tall hat and what looked like a long coat, and though his features were not sharp, he looked very much like the headmaster from the picture she still carried in her bag. If her leg hadn't been in flames, Paige thought, she might have gotten chills.

"When I light the crucible, I need you all to repeat the spell one more time." Duane pulled a lighter out of his pocket and flicked it to start a flame. If the mare knew what was coming, he didn't react. Duane knelt down and aimed the flame at the mashed ingredients inside the crucible. "Now!"

"*Trapiwch y cythraul cysgu!*"

With a loud moan, the mare finally reacted, reaching up as if begging for help from someone in the heavens. And then he slowly started getting smaller, as if he were being sucked into the floor. When he was gone, so was the fire on Paige's pants.

"Oh, thank God," Paige breathed, heaving a heavy sigh. Her pants were charred in places but, surprisingly, were still intact. Greg ran to her and put an arm around her, his relief also palpable.

"So we're done? We did it?" Garrett asked, looking around the stage at all the faces. The hopefulness that filled his eyes and voice made Duncan a bit sad to have to shake his head.

"Nope. But that was important. We sent the sleep demon back to Hell. Now it's time for the puppeteer," Duncan explained.

And then, as if to punctuate his words, a large

gust of wind swept across the stage and blew every candle out. The laughter Paige thought she might have heard earlier now engulfed them, covering them like a tarp above their heads.

Garrett was surprised at Duncan's calm demeanor when he asked Duane, "Do we need to relight the candles?"

Expressionlessly, Duane responded, "It's a different spell anyway."

"What's going on?" Garrett asked, instinctively covering his head to shield himself from the laughter above him.

"It's the puppeteer," Nelson explained. "He's not going to make it easy on us. He's been controlling everything, including the demon, from the start."

"What does that even mean?" Greg asked, looking around as he did.

Nelson shook his head. "Powerful spirits never go down without a fight."

"What?" Greg asked, but no one needed to answer. Flames began shooting up throughout the stage, burning the symbols Duane had drawn to fight the mare.

"My stage!" Garrett yelled, shocked at the sight before him. Anthony stood there with his mouth hanging wide open, his worst fears about to be realized. He was overcome with panic, but he couldn't even move. He stood there paralyzed with the realization that they had failed. And that he would be a victim after all.

They were going to burn.

But Duane was unfazed. He just kept working feverishly, a race to finish this before the whole building went up in flames. He followed the instructions in the book, drawing symbols in the very center of the stage until a loud thud that shook the stage broke his concentration. The echoing laughter stopped abruptly.

Reginald Henriksen, the puppeteer, stood before him.

Duane looked up at the specter before him, slowly taking in his boots, his dark pants, his cape, all the way to his brooding face.

And he was furious.

Duane was about to draw another symbol on the ground when the puppeteer lifted an arm and backhanded Duane across the face, knocking him back and the chalk out of his hand. Clearly seeing Duane as the biggest threat, the puppeteer stalked him as he slid back from the blow and lifted him by the front of his hoodie.

"I have an idea," Duncan stated, nowhere near matching the panic Garrett and Anthony were feeling, but there was an urgency to his tone. Clearly Duncan didn't love watching Duane be accosted by the powerful spirit.

Duncan grabbed the spellbook that lay open on the stage where Duane had been working. In two steps, he leapt off the front of the stage. Anticipating his plan, Paige also grabbed the duffel bag, the crucible, and the chalk Duane had dropped, and followed Duncan off the stage. With a swift swipe of his arm, Duncan knocked back (and over) the tables nearest the stage.

And they continued setting up the spell.

The puppeteer saw what was happening and turned his head toward Paige and Duncan working quickly on the floor in front of the stage.

"Duncan, hurry!" Duane shouted, even as he dangled from the puppeteer's grip. Duane's outburst caught the spirit's attention and he retaliated by tossing Duane toward the back of the stage. He hit it hard and fell to the floor in a heap. Nelson ran to him to make sure he was okay, and they both watched as the puppeteer now marched toward Duncan and Paige, with her half-burnt pants.

But he only took three heavy steps before he froze where he stood. He tried to continue his advance on Duncan and Paige, but he was unable to move. Something held him where he stood.

"Looks like the spell is working," Nelson stated, adjusting his glasses.

But Anthony, from his vantage point, could see tiny lights all around the puppeteer. "It's not the spell.

The boys are holding him."

Garrett came up behind Anthony to see what he was referring to. And, as if on cue, the glowing boy on the end slowly came into view, materializing before them. It was the same boy that had hidden under the stage that first night, complete with bowtie. And instead of crying, he turned to Garrett and Anthony and smiled, his arms still clutching the puppeteer to hold him in place as the puppeteer pulled and fought to get free.

"Well, I'll be...," was all Garrett could muster.

"It's much easier to bully one small boy than the whole group at once, I guess," Anthony stated and then nodded to the boy, thanking him and all his friends for their help.

"And maybe they're sick of being minions and realized they outnumber him," Greg added. Anthony nodded. It was really awe-inspiring to see the children fighting off the puppeteer who was so powerful he could throw Duane.

"I need a candle," Duncan called up to anyone

on the stage.

Garrett looked around his feet and saw a tealight candle not too far from where he stood. It was unlit, so he picked it up and stuck the wick in a small patch of the fire burning his stage. He handed the lit candle to Duncan's outstretched arm.

And the flame was the last piece of the spell. As they chanted the final words and lit the ingredients in the crucible, the puppeteer disappeared. Unlike the mare, who had slowly disappeared, moaning the whole time, the puppeteer was gone in a flash. One moment the boys were holding him, and then he was gone. And all the patches of fire on the stage went out with him.

Garrett didn't even try to hide his relief. He sighed so heavily it almost echoed like the puppeteer's laughter had previously.

"We're not done," Anthony said, looking at Paige. "We can't leave the boys stuck and alone."

She nodded in understanding and hopped back up on stage, standing next to the young bartender and college student. This was as much a part of the job as stopping the sleep demon.

"Boys." Paige spoke calmly and directly to the ghosts who stood in front of her, like a teacher would. "You are now free. The headmaster isn't coming back and you can go to the light. Join your families. They're waiting for you."

Nothing happened. A dozen orbs, some more visibly human spirits than others, still floated on the stage.

"Why aren't they leaving?" Greg asked.

"Is the headmaster not really gone?" Garrett added, a trace of concern lacing his words.

"They're just afraid. They've been under his control for more than a century," Paige explained.

"They were abandoned, Paige," Nelson explained. When she looked at him in confusion, he continued. "This was a boys' home. I doubt they knew their families well, if they even had any to speak of in the first place."

Paige frowned, remembering that Nelson was right. These boys only really had each other.

"They also may not realize they're dead." Duncan hopped back up on the stage. "We've seen that before."

Paige opened her mouth to respond but stopped suddenly when she heard the sound of rustling back in the darkest corner of the nightclub's tables—where they'd done the powder test during the initial investigation. A loud crash echoed throughout the establishment when a chair fell over suddenly.

And Miles came stumbling toward the stage. "Dolores will take 'em."

"Have you been here the whole time?" Garrett asked his best patron.

Miles nodded as Duane blurted out, "Who the hell is Dolores?"

"Meh wife." He stumbled backward a bit, but then found his footing and added with a huge grin, "Meh guardian angel."

Duncan smiled at Miles' prideful face. "That sounds like the perfect plan. Let Dolores take them."

They couldn't see Dolores, but Paige was

almost certain she could sense her. What they saw were dozens of brightly lit orbs slowly disappearing from the stage. One by one, their spirits seemed to fade until the only people left on the stage appeared to be the living ones.

And a wash of calm physically altered the thickness of the air. They could actually feel the difference from before they'd started the ceremony.

With the haunting seemingly behind them, Duncan took stock of the aftermath—and it wasn't pretty. There was fire damage throughout the stage and a broken table or two. "I'm sorry, Garrett. I had no idea it would come to this."

Garrett stomped on a single remaining hot pocket of flame and then walked over to Duncan and patted him brusquely on the back. "It's okay. I have insurance. How I'm going to explain everything to them, I have no idea, but things do happen in a nightclub."

Duncan laughed at his perspective, pushing his long, chestnut-colored bangs out of his eyes as he did so.

And then Paige fainted.

"Paige!" Greg yelled and ran to her side. The whole ordeal had finally gotten to her.

"We've got to get her to a hospital," Anthony blurted.

And Duncan, Nelson and Duane all stared at each other. They'd been bitten, scratched, thrown and even choked at cases gone by, but this was the first time one of them had ever needed a hospital. How bad were her burns?

Lifting her up as if she weighed next to nothing, Duncan instructed his team, "Then let's get her to a hospital. Now."

Chapter 13 – The Mark of the Mare

"Where am I?" Paige blinked her eyes as she woke up in a hospital bed. The lights were dimmed, but the constant beeping of some machine was annoying her out of her stupor.

Greg sat at her side and squeezed her hand. "You gave us quite a scare."

Paige looked around the room, but no one else was there. "What happened? Where is everyone?"

"You have first degree burns up and down your leg, which are surprisingly minor considering how long you were on fire. The doctor thinks you fainted from the smoke inhalation. Regardless, you're going to be just fine."

To confirm his words, Paige lifted her white hospital blanket and inspected her burnt leg. It was red and angry, but not the marred flesh she'd expected to see. There was, however, a strange birthmark-looking dark spot near her hip. She knew for a fact that it hadn't been there before.

Greg stood and leaned over to kiss Paige's forehead. "As to your other question, they're all here. Even Garrett and Anthony. No one wanted to leave you." He walked over to the door and indicated they could all come back into the hospital room. "She's awake."

"Paige! Glad to see you're okay." Duncan beamed at his old friend as he led the team back into Paige's hospital room. Duncan was a kindhearted, open-minded big teddy bear of a man, but in spite of all that, he'd never had a ton of close friends or family. And Paige, whom he'd known since she was a young, bubbly co-ed, was both friend *and* family to him. His parents had never given him any siblings, but he'd found one instead. And the relief he felt at seeing her essentially unharmed after everything she'd been through on this case was overwhelming.

And they kept piling in. Behind Greg and

Duncan came Nelson, then a hoodie-covered Duane, followed by Anthony and Garrett. Paige smiled at their support. They gathered around her bed, Greg at her head. He slipped his hand in hers once more.

"Do you have any pain?" Nelson asked, true concern etched across his face. Paige was like a sister to all of them, and it was never fun to see one of their team get seriously hurt.

But Paige shook her head. "No, just a little tender."

"The doctor said it will be like a bad sunburn. They gave her an ointment and are hydrating her, but pending the results of a chest x-ray to check if she had any damage to her lungs from the smoke, she'll be cleared to go this morning," Greg explained. And Paige listened as intently as the others, since this was also her first time hearing it all.

Anthony reached out and placed a hand gently on her foot from where he stood at the end of the bed. "That's amazing that after how long your pants were on fire, you aren't really that hurt."

"Warlock magic," Nelson answered, as if that said it all. But Paige ignored Nelson because she was staring at Anthony's arm.

"What's that?" Paige blurted, pointing at the birthmark-looking spot. She could see it from where she lay and it looked strangely reminiscent of the one that had appeared on her own hip.

"Oh, this?" Anthony twisted his wrist so he could get a look at the spot. "I don't really know. I just noticed it since we've been at the hospital. I've never had it before tonight."

Duncan rubbed his chin. "Huh. That's strange."

"What's stranger—" Paige started to peel back her covers, but then decided against exposing her legs to a roomful of men. "—is that I have one just like it on my hip."

"It's not strange," Duane said stoically. "It's the mark of the mare. I read it in the spellbook."

"Were you going to say something about it to us?" Greg asked.

Duane stared at Greg for a moment before

answering, "Nope."

"So what does that mean? The mark of the mare?" Duncan asked.

Duane shrugged. "It means they're cursed. I don't know any details."

Anthony groaned and Paige said, "I knew this wasn't over."

"But how is this possible?" Garrett exclaimed. "The mare is gone. The headmaster is gone. The boys crossed over with Miles' wife. How is this still happening?"

Duncan, Paige and Nelson all turned their heads to Duane, leaving it to him to explain. Duane rolled his eyes, but then complied. "The way elemental magic works is that to get something you have to have something taken in return. The price for the spell that freed the Olive was the curse on Paige and Anthony."

"So what's going to happen to her?" Greg almost shouted at Duane.

"I. Don't. Know," Duane responded.

Paige squeezed Greg's hand in an effort to calm

and comfort him. "It's okay, honey. This happens sometimes. We just have to research what we're dealing with and find a way to undo the curse."

Greg's mind was circling back to the fact that Paige shouldn't be doing this—shouldn't be putting herself in harm's way all the time. "This happens sometimes? How often are we talking?"

But before anyone could respond, an elderly gentleman with kind eyes and a stethoscope around his neck waltzed in. "Well, you have quite the fan club, Miss Green."

Greg cleared his throat. "It's Parker now. Mrs. Parker."

"I haven't had the chance to legally change my name yet," Paige shrugged sheepishly.

The doctor smiled warmly. "Then congratulations are in order on two fronts. Your chest x-ray is clear, your burns are superficial. We can begin the discharge process now. I'm happy to have a good ending to your visit to my emergency room."

"Me, too," Paige smiled back.

"Thank you, Dr. Carlson," Greg answered.

The doctor nodded to Greg but then turned back to Paige with a twinkle in his eye. "Now, you take care of yourself, you hear me? I don't want to see you again."

Paige really liked this guy. He reminded her of Santa Claus, if Santa had become a doctor. "I mean this in the best way possible, but I really hope to never see you again either, Dr. Carlson."

"Thatta girl," he said with a wink as he left the room.

When he was out of earshot, Duane muttered, "Dirty ole man."

"So, what's the plan? How do we stop the curse?" Greg brought it back to the matter that consumed his thoughts, asking all the faces in the room and hoping one of them had an answer.

"My guess is we have quite a bit of information at our fingertips in that spellbook." Duncan ran his fingers through his bangs and then let his hands sit on top of his head. "Where is it, Duane?"

"Back at the Olive," Duane answered.

"You left it out of your sight?" Paige asked.

"We were done with spells. Didn't think we'd need it at the hospital." Duane stared at Paige darkly, so she stuck her tongue out at him.

"Then, Greg, you stay here with Paige while she gets discharged from the hospital," Duncan instructed, "and we'll head back to the Olive to see what we can learn about the mark of the mare. Meet us back there as soon as you can."

Greg nodded in affirmation, but Paige responded with, "Duncan? There's something else." Everyone held their breath waiting for Paige to explain further. "My mark is...tingling. I think that means something."

Garrett nudged Anthony. "What about you? Any tingling?"

Anthony stared at his mark again. "It's like a strange burning sensation."

"So what does this mean?" Greg asked again. He had so many questions and was so filled with worry, he was wringing his hands, not sure what to do with his excess energy.

"I think it means—" Nelson adjusted his glasses nervously. "—that we need to get back to the Olive *now.*"

When all except Greg and Paige were back at the Olive, they wasted no time in grabbing the spellbook and looking for information on the mark of the mare. Duncan held the book, but Duane directed him to the page near the mare-binding spell that showed the mark of the mare as a drawing. It was shaped like a warped upside-down heart.

"Anthony," Duncan practically shouted as he swung the book around to compare the marking on Anthony's skin to the drawing in the spellbook that depicted the mark of the mare. Anthony raised his sleeve to his elbow so they could all get a better look.

"It's pretty close," Duncan announced. It wasn't identical to the drawing—Anthony's was wider, rounder—but they were similar enough that it didn't seem like a coincidence. Anthony had had a run-in with the mare and now bore a mark oddly similar to the mark of the mare? It was proof enough for Duncan.

"What does it say about how to get rid of it?" Garrett leaned in, trying to decipher for himself, never mind that he'd never used a spellbook a day in his life.

"It doesn't that I remember," Duane stated.

"The mark of the mare," Duncan read aloud, "indicates a soul's binding to its master. Once made, the mark of the mare can be used to feed on the soul without the need of dreamstate."

"It sounds a lot like the old witch's marks." Nelson straightened his glasses. "You know, how back in the day if you were accused of being a witch, they thought they could tell if you were one by looking for a mark somewhere on the skin. The belief being that Satan could feed on the witch's soul through that mark. Of course, those witches gave their souls willingly." He cleared his throat. "Or they were just birthmarks and the poor women got burnt at the stake anyway."

"Okay. I have a mark that lets the mare feed on me.   I guess that explains the strange tingling sensation," Anthony stated wide-eyed. "How do I make it go away?"

"Nelson? Any theories?" Duncan asked.

Nelson shook his head. "This is my first encounter with a sleep demon. But I do know a few websites on the Occult that might have a clue or two."

"Duane." Duncan shoved the spellbook into Duane's hands. "You flip through here and see if there is any counter spell to anything even closely resembling a mare or witchcraft or demons of any kind. We can try it even if it's a stretch."

Duane nodded and then placed the spellbook on the stage as he stood on the floor in front of it, hoodie up, leafing through every page.

Garrett shook his head. "This is nuts. Are all your cases like this?"

Duncan shook his head. "Yours is the first of its kind."

"Lovely," Garrett said sarcastically, letting his arms flop dramatically at his sides.

"But don't worry, Anthony." Duncan laid a

comforting hand on the young man's shoulder. "We're not leaving until we've gotten rid of your curse."

"I know." Anthony stared at the weird mark on his wrist. "I know you wouldn't leave Paige like this."

"We won't leave *either* of you," Duncan responded.

"Aha! I think I got something," Nelson announced. His excitement filled the room and he bounced on the balls of his feet as Paige so often did. "There's a message forum about witch's marks and curses."

"And? What'd they say?" Garrett asked. He was eager for this all to be over with, so he could go back to his life of quiet days and endless nights running a nightclub in Seattle. He wanted music on the stage and happy patrons in the seats. He wanted his biggest worry to again be putting Miles in a cab at the end of the night. He thought back to how that used to annoy him—and how it would never bother him again once this was all over. In fact, he looked forward to it and hoped he'd be carrying a drunk Miles to a cab once again very soon.

"A witch hopped on and answered a few who thought they may have marks," Nelson explained. "She says you have to give them something in your place. There's no way to just get the curse off you. I guess it's like Duane said: one thing in place of another in elemental magic."

"So, I have to transfer the curse to someone else?" Anthony asked, the horror plainly written on his face. "That's awful."

"The witch said *something*, right? Not someone?" Duncan looked pointedly at Nelson.

Before he answered, Nelson looked at the webpost he had pulled up on his smartphone. "Yes. That's right. Something in your place."

"What else has a soul that it can suck?" Garrett asked.

"If it works, who cares if the mare can't suck any more souls," Duncan answered.

"This spell might work," Duane announced, lifting the open book and turning to the team.

"Deflecting a curse."

"Isn't it too late to deflect?" Anthony asked. "It's already cursed me."

"The whole point of the spell is to deflect the curse on you...— " Duane looked at Nelson. "—and *transfer* it to someone or something else."

The silence that followed Duane's statement hung heavy in the air all around them. It was early morning, another all-nighter, and they were exhausted. They had stopped the mare from its continual destruction of the Seattle community every few years in a countdown pattern. But now it was even more personal than the usual haunting of someone's home, or even bar. Ghosts were once people. They all knew how to deal with ghosts and people.

But deflecting curses? This was next level.

"Anyone have any better ideas?" Duncan asked, looking around the room.

No one said anything in response.

Instead, the heavy front door to the Olive burst open and Paige bounced in with an explosion of energy. There was a dusting of water droplets in her short brown hair and she looked like she'd been up all night, but otherwise, she seemed back to her usual bubbly self. "Let's do this!"

Greg followed her, much more subdued. He looked like Garrett felt. He was ready for all of this to be done. His shoulders slumped and there were bags under his eyes. He said nothing as he closed the Olive entrance door behind himself on the way in.

"You don't even know what 'this' is, yet," Duane answered.

Paige shrugged as she practically skipped toward the group that gathered near the stage. "If it frees me from the curse, I'm in."

Anthony stood up straight. "I'm in too. Let's deflect."

"Deflect?" Paige asked, her smile faltering a tad.

"You can't just undo the curse, Paige," Nelson explained. "You have to transfer it."

"But we've undone dozens of curses before. Spell, counter spell. Right?" Paige asked.

"This one's a bit different. There's no way to just make it go away," Nelson responded.

"So Duane found a curse deflection spell in the spellbook and we were just discussing whether or not to try it when you waltzed in," Duncan added.

"Oh," was all Paige could say.

"Is it fast? Because I would like to curl up in my bed and sleep until noon without worrying that something was going to suck my soul while I did it. And I don't think that's too much to ask," Greg said.

Duane just rolled his eyes.

"What do we deflect to?" Paige asked.

At first, no one answered. But then Nelson announced, "I think I have an idea."

Chapter 14 – Curse Deflection

"Let's just not use the stage," Garrett suggested as Duane placed the duffel bag there. "I can't take any more damage to it."

Without responding, Duane lifted the duffel bag and used it instead to knock over two more tables near the front of the Olive, by the stage. Garrett cringed but let it go. He'd have to spend some time assessing all the damage from this night anyway. And he doubted it would be anything but painful.

"Just hurry, Duane. It's tingling again," Paige stated.

"You don't even want to know what that means," Anthony told her.

"I've been doing this long enough that I can take a wild guess. And you're right, I don't want the details," Paige smiled. Anthony was impressed she could still be smiling, cursed as they were.

He'd never been cursed before and he could honestly say he hoped he never was again.

"I really hope this works," Garrett said. It was the only thing running through his mind: severe doubt in the spell's prospects which he was trying to shove down with optimistic words. His heart wasn't really in it, though.

"It will," Duncan said with a bravado he didn't actually feel. He put the deflection spell's likelihood of removing the curse at 50/50 best case. Nelson gave him a look that said he knew Duncan was overcompensating, but he thankfully said nothing.

Duane worked on the floor, setting up the tealight candles just as he'd done earlier in the day. This time they were lined up in the shape of an ocean wave's profile. Along the perimeter he sprinkled bay leaves and coriander. Over his shoulder he spoke to Nelson. "This is where I need to put the receptacle."

"All right, Nelson." Duncan gestured at his fellow investigator. "You're up."

Nelson cleared his throat and then said, "Remember earlier when we trapped the mare? Pull up that footage."

Duane stood up and walked over to the camera on the stage. It had been mounted since the previous ceremony and was just sitting there since then. He took the camera down and watched the viewfinder as he rewound to the trapped mare in the center of the stage. Duane then walked over to Nelson and handed him the camera.

"Yes. This. See here?" Nelson paused what he was looking at and handed the camera to Duncan.

"Oh. I hadn't noticed that in real time," Duncan answered.

"What is it?" Paige asked. She wanted to know, but she didn't want to squeeze in with Duncan and Nelson to watch the tiny screen.

"The boys' ghosts had rats at their feet," Duncan explained.

Paige shook her head violently. "No. No way. I'm not passing the curse to any living things."

"I don't think they're living things," Nelson said.

"What do you think they are?" Paige asked.

"I think they might also be ghosts," Nelson answered.

Garrett groaned. "So, I also have ghost rats? This is unreal. Is there anything *not* haunting my club?"

"My theory is that they are a residual haunting—more like a memory for the boys than an actual ghost infestation," Nelson explained.

"How exactly do you plan to use a residual haunting of a pet rat in a spell?" Duane asked, skepticism written plainly on his face.

"Well, I was thinking." Nelson placed the camera gently on the floor near the crest of the wavelike pattern of candles. "Since they are just a memory that we only have to evoke said memory."

"It just said we have to give something in return. There were no specifics. Maybe a memory is good enough," Duncan stated, hands on his hips.

"I think it's a longshot, at best," Duane

muttered.

"It's nonsense," Garrett said, looking around the room waiting for someone to say, 'Just kidding.'

"I say we do it," Greg answered, more committed than anyone expected him to be. "Worst case it doesn't work. We try something else."

"I like that attitude, honey," Paige beamed. "And best case, no other living creature has to be harmed by transferring this curse."

"I agree that it's a bit of a stretch, but it's a curse. Curses are intangible things, and so are these ghost rats. At least, that's the basis for my theory," Nelson explained, rubbing his chin. He didn't sound any more confident than Duncan, but no one argued. No one was voicing any brighter ideas, either.

"Okay. Ghost rats it is, then." Duane pulled his black hoodie over his bald head and knelt on the floor. "I need you all in a circle around me and the candles."

With heavy feet, they all complied. The air felt smothering, thick as it was with the skepticism everyone felt at the prospect of transferring the curse to a memory. Duane lit all the candles and opened the spellbook wide. He mixed lavender with coriander and sage, grinding them into a paste. Just before he recited the spell, he flicked his lighter and set fire to the concoction.

From past experience, Paige grabbed Duncan's hand on the one side and Greg's on the other and began humming—although it escaped no one's notice that she took a step back when the lighter came out. Not knowing what else to do, everyone else besides Duane joined in. They were humming and swaying, hand in hand in a circle, when Duane recited the words from the incantation. It didn't say how many times he had to say the words, so he repeated them three times since that was what he'd found in the past to be the typical amount needed to get results.

"It worked!" Paige shouted and pointed at the camera and candles in front of a kneeling Duane.

"The curse transferred to the ghost rats?" Garrett could barely hide his disbelief. True, he had very little experience with these things, but the whole transfer-curses-with-common-spices thing was hard for him to swallow. Never mind the fact they were transferring to a ghost within a recorded video.

This whole experience was a suspension in disbelief from the moment he saw the bony hand. And it hadn't gotten any better.

"Well, no," Paige frowned. "But it transferred to the camera! See?" She lifted the camera and angled the side to show everyone. "The mark of the mare." Sure enough, the rounded upside-down heart symbol was etched into the side of the camera.

"What?" Duncan grabbed the camera from Paige to see for himself.

"Good enough for me. The mark is gone from my wrist," Anthony stated, lifting his arm in the air to show everyone the lack of mark. He made no attempt to disguise his relief.

"What about yours, Paige?" Greg came up to her side. "Is your mark gone?"

Paige averted her eyes as she tried to discern how she would inspect her hip without this gathering of men watching her lower her pants. When she came up with the solution, she plopped the cursed camera in Greg's hand and marched to the bar area. Once safely out of eyesight of everyone else, she inspected her hip. Red, sore, tender. But no weird mark.

"Also, gone," Paige stated.

Garrett shook his head. His long, blonde hair brushed his shoulders with the movement. "No. No way. This was way too easy. There's gotta be a catch."

Duncan looked at his nervous client. "Sometimes we just get lucky."

"Who cares? If it worked, it worked," Greg said, relieved that his wife wasn't going to burn or levitate in her sleep. "But what do we do with this?" He held out the camera which now held the curses.

"I'm not sure," Duncan started, but Duane walked over to Greg and yanked the camera out of his hands. Greg was fairly certain he didn't like this bald-headed tattooed guy.

And then Duane startled the whole group when he threw the camera with full force straight at the ground, shattering it into a thousand pieces.

"Not what I was going to propose," Nelson said, adjusting his glasses, "but I suppose it gets the job done."

Chapter 15 – Cleaning Up

Garrett swept up the pieces of shattered camera, table splinters, and ashes from the floor of the Olive. After removing the curse, they had all gone their separate ways to sleep and recover from the night's events. Even though it was afternoon now, very little natural light was making its way in due to the rain and clouds blocking the sun.

It seemed fitting to Garrett that the day after they fought a centuries-old curse on Seattle, the city would want to wash it all away with a rainstorm.

While Garrett was glad everything was over, he hung his shoulders in defeat when he looked at the destruction all around him. He wouldn't be able to reopen for weeks.

When his pile had gotten large enough to remove, he ducked into his office to grab the dustpan.

He hadn't yet reemerged when he heard the main door to the Olive open and close. Of course, he hadn't locked it because he knew the investigators were going to stop by on their way out of town, but he figured they might call first. Dustpan in hand, he peeked his head around the doorjamb to see who his visitor might be.

And he smiled when he saw that it was Miles.

But Miles looked so different. He was cleaned up, washed and shaven. His eyes were clear and bright. He was most decidedly sober. Garrett had never seen this version of Miles. But he liked it.

"Miles." He smiled sincerely at his patron. "You look good. To what do I owe this pleasure?"

"I came to thank you." Miles's voice was clear and strong. "Now that Dolores has crossed over and the monster in my dreams is gone, I'm ready to move on." Miles shook his head at his past ordeal. "Ya know, last night was my first good night's sleep in a long time."

"I can believe it." Garrett walked over to the tables in front of the bar—the ones that hadn't been smashed. "But why thank me? I did nothing. Your wife did more for us last night than I've ever done."

Miles smiled. His skin was leathery with years of a hard life, but there was a true happiness on his face that Garrett had never seen before. "I had demons of my own to battle. And as I did, you were always here for me. I wasn't ready then, but I'm ready now. I'm done drinking. Quittin' cold turkey!"

Garrett half-smiled as he thought about all the times he'd carried Miles to the car. "I love hearing that," and even as he said it to one of his best customers, he knew it was true. "When we're back open for business, come in for a soda or something instead."

"Actually..." Miles cocked an eyebrow as he let the word linger on his lips. "I was wondering if I might be able to play every now and again. At the Olive. I have a few musician friends and we're starting up a group like old times. They've been asking me for a while, but I hadn't been ready. You can call it Throwback Thursdays or something?"

There was a twinkle and lightness to his eyes that Garrett had never seen before. Miles had always been in a deep, dark place. But getting back to his love of music? Garrett loved the sound of that. "Deal. But only if you let me play a set or two with you." He winked at Miles, and Miles laughed.

"You can sure try!" Miles shook his head at the young bar owner. They laughed together and the feeling was so liberating, for both of them.

The front door opened again and in towered Duncan. He shook off the raindrops as he lowered the hood of his jacket. He smiled, wide and genuine, when he saw Garrett and a much-cleaned-up version of Miles. "Hey, you two."

"Duncan. Hi. Heading out of town?" Garrett asked.

Duncan watched Garrett kneel down and brush the pile of wooden bits and ash onto his dustpan. "We were planning to, but we can stay if you need help here. I feel bad for trashing your place."

"Nah. Dead boys? Demons? Curses? Not my

thing. But this I can handle." Garrett stood up and emptied his dustpan into a large trash can he'd placed centrally to make it easier to clean up. He then placed the dustpan on one of the tables that hadn't been destroyed in last night's battle. "Go ahead and hit the road. I believe your work here is done."

"It is," Miles added. "That monster's been haunting me for years, but last night? Finally gone."

"Where's everyone else?" Garrett made an effort to see around the large investigator.

"Well, Paige and Greg are finally starting their honeymoon, so they went to see some sights," Duncan explained.

"Honeymoon?" Garrett didn't even attempt to disguise his shock.

"Believe it or not, yes. That's Paige for ya." Duncan smiled. "And Nelson and Duane already hit the road in the P.I.L. van." He aimed a thumb at the door to gesture just exactly how gone they were.

"Do you think there'll be any residual...damage from the soul-sucking of Paige and Anthony?" Garrett had to ask.

Duncan shook his head. "Truthfully, I don't know. But we can do some more research when we get home. I hope not."

Garrett looked around. "Well, I've been here all morning and so far the only mess is the one you can actually see with your naked eye. If something's lurking, it's definitely staying quiet for now."

"Oh! That reminds me." Duncan dug around his jacket pocket. "Burn this and fan it around your club. It's sage and it gets rid of negative energy. If anything is lurking, this will keep it at bay."

He handed it to Garrett, who seemed to take it eagerly. Any skepticism he'd had before all this was now clearly gone.

"And, of course," Duncan added, "if you do have any supernatural experiences, call me. We can always come back."

"You know I will." Garrett extended his hand and Duncan shook it. "But I feel like Paige did with the doctor. I hope I never have to see you again. Take care."

"And you," Duncan nodded with a smile. He completely understood the sentiment. He then turned to Miles. "And you, too, Miles. Take care."

"I'm right as rain," Miles beamed, and Duncan had to silently agree.

"Then it looks like my work here is done," Duncan said, clasping his hands together.

"I think it is, Duncan. Drive safely back to Cali," Garrett responded.

When Duncan was back in his beat-up old Chevy, Garrett went back to the arduous task before him, but he noticed Miles didn't leave. He watched as Miles began picking up large pieces of broken furniture and placing it in the trash can. And then, owner and patron both silently continued cleaning up the physical mess left by the paranormal battle.

"Let's go to the Woodland Park Zoo." Paige pointed at the map in the location of the zoo.

"More than Pike Place?" Greg asked.

Paige shrugged. "There's a lot of ghosts at Pike Place, or so I've heard. And I'm on vacation."

Greg regarded her a minute before saying, "Zoo it is. Do we wait for it to stop raining?"

"Nah. We have to live like the locals. If you let a little rain stop you in Seattle, you might never go outside."

Paige continued packing up her day bag. She was used to carrying everything with her when she was on a case, and she couldn't help herself now that they were tourists. She packed a notebook, a snack, a water bottle, an extra pair of socks in case her feet got soaked... But she stopped and turned around when she felt the heat of Greg staring at her intently. "What?"

"I hated it. Watching you catch on fire. That was the most horrible thing I've ever seen in my life."

Paige waved off his concern. Not because she didn't agree—it had been a horrible experience for her too—but because she didn't want to think about it on her honeymoon. And she didn't want him to get overly concerned again, because that meant he would try and stop her from investigating.

And that would most definitely put a damper on the day.

"You get used to it. We get cursed and thrown and stuff all the time. But we always resolve it. That's our job." Paige tossed her bag on her shoulder in emphasis of her point. She was ready to go.

And she didn't want to talk about it anymore.

Greg walked slowly toward her. He grabbed the bag from her shoulder and placed it on the floor at her feet. "You didn't let me finish. I get it now."

Paige stood there silently staring for a beat. He couldn't possibly be agreeing with her, could he? She didn't want to dare let her heart dream that he was finally supporting her in this. "Get what?"

"Fighting the sleep demon was scary and intense, and it sucked you in and that was awful. But you really made a difference. Not just for Garrett and Anthony, but for all those lost boys. So I get it. You face the danger and the fear so you can help people. And the souls." Greg lifted his shoulders in a small shrug. "You're kinda like a firefighter in that way."

Paige huffed a laugh. No one had ever accused them of being everyday heroes before. It seemed like hyperbole. But she'd take the compliment from someone who had been so skeptical before. "So, you're supportive now?"

"Supportive? I'd like to go on cases every now and again if you'll have me." Greg beamed, a true ear-to-ear smile. "I guess I actually really enjoyed myself."

Paige threw her arms around his neck and squeezed. Still clutching his neck in an embrace, she said, "I had decided to live with compartmentalizing my life. P.I.L. on one side and you on the other. But you have no idea how thrilled I am to not have to do that."

"And you shouldn't have to. I'm sorry I ever questioned it."

She hopped back on the balls of her feet as she pulled away from their embrace. Her short brown hair bounced around her face and happiness radiated from every pore. "The zoo?"

Greg gestured for her to lead the way. "The zoo."

Paige lifted her daybag back onto her shoulder and she practically skipped out the hotel room door. Greg started to follow her and then looked down at the circled map of Seattle resting on the dresser. He saw the dates scribbled all over the map and remembered all the twists and turns they'd gone through to help Garrett get The Olive Nightclub back.

And he was proud.

He closed the door to the hotel room with the satisfaction that comes from solving a case and giving some souls peace—souls both living and dead.

Chapter 16 – Conan Henriksen's Story

We weren't the only family with talents from the Old World, as warlock magic was known on the East Coast, but it was getting harder and harder to blend in. When Reginald and Dolly decided to head out West, I decided to go with them.

I had heard tales of gold and riches out West, the kind that alter your life forever. And there was nothing keeping me in New York anymore. I had courted a few ladies, but the only woman who had ever truly held my heart was married to my brother.

Where she went, I went.

Reginald was the eldest, so of course he was matched with Dolly. It shattered my heart to watch them unite their lives in holy matrimony, but I never spoke my feelings. Outwardly I supported Reginald completely.

But Dolly kept looking at me. It wasn't just my imagination. She was attracted to me too.

Reginald and I were about as different as two people could be. I was quiet, thoughtful. I enjoyed my solitude. Reginald was outgoing, gregarious, the life of the party. In fact, most people loved Reginald and barely tolerated me. The thought that Dolly might be interested in me when she had Reginald? It was too much to hope.

And yet, hope I did.

So when Reginald announced that he and his young bride were heading out west, I decided to tag along. To find my opportunity. And to stay near my heart's desire: my brother's wife.

Of course, if I had given it a moment's thought I would have realized what a dangerous game I was playing. If Dolly ever told me she loved me too, I would break up a marriage at the very least. And I'd be betraying my own brother.

And at the worst, I'd be risking my brother's wrath. The wrath of a very powerful warlock.

My mother had been the original master of talents from the Old World. From the time we were still in our swaddling clothes, my mother was teaching us about spells, conjurings and encantations. I hadn't thought much about it. It was just part of our lives.

But Reginald had taken to it. He was a natural. And he was passionate, always asking my mom questions and eager to learn more. Sure, it would be a lie to say I hadn't used a little revenge magic here and there in my lifetime. But nothing I ever did was as committed as Reginald.

He'd studied, practiced and perfected. He was a true warlock.

But I never worried once that that would come back to haunt me. It was just a part of who Reginald was. Whether it was foolishness or arrogance, I can only suppose. And I had never laid a hand on Dolly. I had only stolen a few looks of longing and nothing more.

But everything changed when we headed out West.

The trail had been long and painful. My rear end

was covered in sores from interminable days sitting in the wagon. And for some reason, I had imagined a land of milk and honey. I imagined riches overflowing everywhere you turned. I thought even the sun would never stop shining in this new land where opportunity awaited.

But when the trail ended, it was just another dreary forest like the one I'd left behind back East.

A goldminer named Jed that we'd come to know told us to head north if we wanted a chance at a better life. He told us everyone was heading south, and we were late to the gold rush. North was where the new opportunity was waiting, ripe for the taking.

We listened. We headed up to Elliott Bay and soon felt very much at home. And even if we hadn't, we'd have had to stay. The trip across the continent had cost us everything we had.

Reginald found work right away in a lumber mill. He left for work early in the morning and often worked long, hard days. When he got home, he could barely keep his eyes open long enough to eat before he fell asleep. And then the whole day started again.

But I had always been more of an intellectual. Swinging an axe and doing manual labor was never right for my natural talents. So I got a job at a small one-room schoolhouse teaching the local children near our home.

And I had much more time at home with Dolly than Reginald did.

It wasn't something that either of us forced. It was just as natural as the rain that so often fell from the skies. We'd talk in the evenings, and she really enjoyed hearing about my day with the students. I'd often read to her from a book of poetry I loved. She sat across the room from me, at first. And soon, she was kneeling at my feet. And then resting a hand on my knee.

And stolen glances turned to stolen kisses. And it just kept progressing from there. We were connected and in love in a way that Dolly and Reginald never had been. And he was never around. Someone needed to hold her and make her feel secure. I felt very little remorse and no fear. I felt dutiful. I was taking care of

Dolly as she deserved to be taken care of.

But it was very difficult to deny once Dolly realized she was with child. Reginald knew for a fact that it wasn't his. He hadn't been with his wife in the marital sense for months. He never asked directly, and we certainly never admitted it openly, but the truth of it was always there hovering over the three of us like a cloud.

And still, I ignorantly went about my day as if Reginald suspected nothing.

When Joseph was born, all three of us were overjoyed.

He was perfect. His round face and sweet dimples completely convinced me that everything was right with the world. What could be wrong in a union that created such perfection?

As Joseph grew into a healthy and strong little boy, things continued as they'd had since we'd first moved to Elliot Bay. How was I to know that all the while Reginald was plotting his revenge quietly and in the background?

I was so ignorant.   I thought his quiet complacence was acceptance. And it was not.

I could accept that he wanted to curse me. I might even dare to admit I deserved it. But I could never forgive his effortless and ruinous framing of Dolly as a witch. Because there was a small flood? And how easily the townspeople had accepted it. I hated them for that, too.

At least he spared the boy, Joseph. I do think a part of Reginald loved him as much as we all did. Dolly and I would pay the price, but Reginald let Joseph go free. I have always been thankful for that.

But even besmirching Dolly's good name was just a small part of Reginald's plan.

Despite his long hours at the lumber mill, Reginald started spending hours studying spells and incantations every evening.   He would study by candlelight until the wick could barely flicker. Once, Dolly mentioned the candles he was burning through. This was quite the expense for us and there was young Joseph to feed. But Reginald told her he was looking for the way to improve their futures. We all assumed he was setting up a spell to lead us to gold. Or alchemy, where we could make our own gold.

I still never suspected that he was biding his time for revenge on his own brother.

So when the fire came, I was as ignorant as I had always been.

Dolly and I died in the flames, choking on smoke long before our bodies turned to ash. Our little log cabin home burned with the heat of a thousand spells. There was no way to escape it, unless Reginald wanted you to.

Like Joseph.

Two people walked away that day: my son and my brother.

And then Reginald told everyone that he was me and that he had run off after his wife died in the flames! He moved and got a job using my work experience to become a headmaster at a reform school for young boys. And that insult wasn't even the worst he did to me. At least he just let Dolly die. Me? The brother he'd come to hate? He cursed me to become a monster in my afterlife, to match the monster he believed I was in life. He used me to grow in power with the souls I collected.

All because I loved Dolly, he made me his eternal lackey from Hell.

And there was nothing I could do. I was compelled. And I would get so hungry that the only way to satiate my appetite was to suck the souls of sleeping humans. There was no fighting it. I was a demon. A monster. For all eternity. With no opportunity to right my wrongs.

Decades would pass before we could both be stopped and sent to an afterlife devoid of God.

And I now accept my fate for betraying my brother. As long as Dolly and Joseph were spared this curse. As long as they can rest in peace in Heaven.

I will be the monster, so they can fly with the angels.